Guy led Alana onto the dance floor

Taking her in his arms as the band began a slow dreamy number, he held her close, his chin against her mass of silken hair.

Despite herself awareness grew inside her, and she was conscious of his body against hers.

"What are you afraid of?" he asked softly. "Haven't you been this close to a man before?"

She had, but never so vulnerably. The chemistry between them was growing out of control. She had to escape.

But when she tried to pull away from him, she found he was holding her too close to make escape possible. Then the hand on her shoulders dropped lower, bringing her body intimately against his. Staring up at him, her blue eyes were feverish.

"Don't worry," he drawled, "if I do seduce you, it won't be in quite so public a place."

MARGARET PARGETER
is also the author of these

Harlequin Presents

and these
Harlequin Romances

Many of these books are available at your local bookseller.

For a free catalog listing all titles currently available,
send your name and address to:

HARLEQUIN READER SERVICE
1440 South Priest Drive, Tempe, AZ 85281
Canadian address: Stratford, Ontario N5A 6W2

MARGARET PARGETER

prelude to a song

Harlequin Books

TORONTO • NEW YORK • LOS ANGELES • LONDON
AMSTERDAM • PARIS • SYDNEY • HAMBURG
STOCKHOLM • ATHENS • TOKYO • MILAN

Harlequin Presents first edition February 1983
ISBN 0-373-10572-X

Original hardcover edition published in 1982
by Mills & Boon Limited

CHAPTER ONE

THE girl on the train felt apprehensive. She had been almost asleep when the two youths sat down opposite her and began staring.

'Are you on your way to London?' asked one, his eyes travelling boldly over the girl's long wealth of fair hair and what he could see of her slender young figure.

Nervously Alana flushed, and when she didn't answer he persisted brashly, 'Will you be staying long?'

This time when she remained stubbornly silent he glanced knowingly at his companion and laughed. Turning back to her, he said, 'Don't be nervous, darling, we're just being sociable. We'd like to know you better.'

Something in his eyes and voice threw her in a panic. She rose, grabbing hold of her suitcase which had been too heavy for her to lift to the rack above her head. 'Excuse me,' she mumbled, 'I'm with someone.'

'I hadn't noticed,' the other youth jeered. 'Where is he?' he made an exaggerated pretence of looking under the table.

'He—he'll be back any moment.' She regarded them from wide, frightened eyes as she tried to free her case, somehow stuck in the seat against the window.

Neither made any attempt to assist her. 'If you're with someone,' said the bold-eyed one, leaning forward, 'why move? If you do he won't know where to find you, will he? Look,' he grinned ingratiatingly, 'why not be sensible? A pretty girl like you, alone in a big city, is going to need all the friends she can get, and you won't find any better than us.'

'No, thank you.' Alana's clear voice shook, which detracted somewhat from the emphasis she strove for.

The boy sneered, bending nearer, touching her bare arm with a grimy, threatening finger. 'Don't give yourself airs with me, darling. I know your sort.'

The compartment was practically empty. An old man dozed in the seat across the aisle; further along two elderly ladies were also nodding. Then, just as Alana's terrified glance rested on the last unlikely source of help, the carriage door swung open and a man strode through, carrying a couple of cans of beer and a packet of sandwiches.

Her reaction purely instinctive, Alana stumbled to block his path. 'Oh, darling,' she gasped, 'what a time you've been!'

The youths stared then slunk away, immediately disappearing. Alana didn't blame them. The man whom she was clutching was tall and tough-looking, extremely intimidating and probably twice their ages.

He stood entirely still, not uttering a word. The only thing to move about him was his eyebrows, which rose quizzically. She felt compelled to break the uncomfortable silence.

'I'm sorry,' she whispered, 'I do apologise, but it was either you or the communication cord.'

'Next time try the guard,' he advised dryly, releasing himself from her unconsciously clinging hands. 'I don't mind obliging, but there's usually one around.' When she swayed on her feet he glanced at her sharply, then pushing her none too gently back into her seat, he sat down opposite.

'Why didn't I think of that?' she muttered, her head swimming.

He studied her grimly and somehow, crazily, she began feeling trapped by his eyes. They were dark, she thought grey, she couldn't be sure, but as they met hers she felt their impact like a flash of electricity. She was conscious of her own eyes widening as they were caught and held by the disturbing sensation radiating between them. Her stomach churned and her bones seemed to melt. What was it? she wondered with an audibly drawn breath, finding it took an almost physical effort to look away. She was surprised to find she was trembling.

'Thanks for your help, anyway,' she said. 'I won't keep you, I'll be all right now.'

He didn't move. 'Those two lads obviously gave you a fright. I recognise the type. They're like ferrets. Once on the scent they don't give up easily, and they could be back. It'll be no problem to keep you company for a while.'

'But—your luggage?'

'I don't have any.'

Still not completely recovered from the shock she had received, Alana exclaimed dazedly, 'If you've come from the north you must have stayed overnight? What about your pyjamas?'

'I don't wear any.'

'Oh,' she said.

'Ah,' he grinned.

Her cheeks coloured as she realised the incongruous drift of their conversation. She felt terribly embarrassed, not knowing what to say next. Nor did she dare look at him. Somehow she had to get rid of him.

'Won't your wife be wondering where you've got to?'

'I don't have a wife either.'

'You certainly do believe in travelling light!' she observed sharply, unthinkingly.

She sensed his quirk of amusement although she couldn't see it. Why did she not need to look at him to verify her suspicions? Why was she so aware of everything about this man, a complete stranger? It was as if he was some part of herself which had been missing. For heaven's sake! she rebuked herself, thinking the shock she had had must have affected her mind. Of all the silly, impossible things!

'I'm glad to hear you have some spirit left,' he cut through her thoughts sardonically, 'but what's so fascinating about the top of a British Rail table?'

This brought her head up with a jerk and caught off guard her eyes locked with his again.

Although he must have noticed how her hands clenched in silent protest, he refused to let her go. He imprisoned her glance with an ease which warned her that his experience at this kind of game was way beyond hers.

'Blue,' he mused, satisfaction tinging his well modulated voice, 'quite incredibly blue. The only other eyes I've ever known as blue as yours belonged to my mother.'

'Yours are grey,' she heard herself muttering shyly, as if she was in a kind of trance. Vaguely she was conscious of other things about him, his height and breadth, which had scared the two boys, and his dark good looks. He was a cool, very much in command kind of person, at least in his middle thirties, possibly older. No wonder the boys had flown! In his casual attire this man gave the impression of lean, muscled power. His hands, she had noted, as he placed the two cans he carried on the table, also gave the impression of strength above average. She remembered them touching her and shivered.

His sensuous mouth curved in a twisted smile. 'When I was younger, and my mother was still alive, I used to say if I ever met a girl with eyes as blue as hers I'd marry her and have the most beautiful blue-eyed children.'

Again Alana's breath caught. Perhaps he was only teasing her a little for the trouble she had caused him, but she sensed suddenly that he might be infinitely more dangerous than the two youths he had just got rid of. The rays hitting her from his eyes began penetrating deeply. They traced the length of her long, graceful neck to spearhead in twin directions, insolently hitting areas she had scarcely been conscious of before.

Feeling curiously shattered by such a comprehensive surveillance, Alana was forced to bite her lip to prevent another gasp escaping, and her eyes, which appeared to be so intriguing her mysterious rescuer, darkened. She became too aware of his glance resting speculatively on the rounded curves of her slight body and of the growing interest in them. As he was a bachelor she supposed he felt free to look at women as long as he liked, but she wished he would stop looking at her. She wasn't altogether fond of a churning stomach and a heart which responded to a complete stranger as if it was threatening to break all speed records!

Her fine white fingers tautened as his breath rasped and she knew a belated indignation. How could she, Alana Hurst, a level-headed girl of twenty, be allowing her imagination to run away with her in such a fashion? In a few minutes this man would go and she would never see him again.

Managing to insert a note of crispness into her voice, she exclaimed. 'I'm sure you would soon have dozens of blue-eyed children if you married every blue-eyed girl you met!'

'I'm not quite that ambitious,' he smiled, removing his glance from her.

She wasn't sure that she appreciated his ability to return to normal quite so easily. Something had been smouldering between them and he had turned the pressure down deliberately, she fancied, then chided herself again for fancying so much.

'Will this be your first visit to London?' he asked

before she could comment on his last observation.

'No. I've been there before, with my parents,' she replied. Sometimes, when they were taking her back to school, and had been able to afford it, they had stayed in the capital for a few days, But she needn't tell him this.

'The first time on your own, then?'

'Yes.' He was so astute he would know if she didn't tell the truth.

He shoved a can of beer towards her and the top popped as she automatically opened it and the air rushed in. The old man across the way gave a grunt in his sleep and the train emitted a high-pitched whine as it raced furiously towards the distant city.

'You're on holiday, perhaps?'

'No.' The beer was marvellously cold running down her throat, which suddenly felt parched.

Steadily he stared at her. 'You've a remarkable vocabulary. If you're trying to tell me to mind my own business, why not come right out with it?' When she flushed guiltily, he added suavely, 'I'm only trying to be kind.'

Did he know anything about kindness? She was conscious for the first time of a certain hardness in his powerfully moulded features, of a hard, controlled but sensuous mouth. The deeply cleft chin below it, set in a tough-looking jaw, indicated a man used to fighting battles and winning them. Again a shiver ran down through her and she flinched.

'I'm sorry,' her voice rushed with embarrassment as her glance rose to meet the slightly enquiring irony in his, 'I'm not on holiday. I shouldn't mind if I was, but I'm looking for work.'

'Ah,' he said, and she wondered how he managed to convey so much cynicism with that one little word. 'So the bright lights attract you, do they, like a moth to the flames?'

'No, you're wrong,' she stared at the table because it was easier, 'it's a case of necessity.'

'That's a big word,' he said dryly. 'People get confused about it. Are you sure you know what it means?'

'Oh, yes, Mr . . .' as he didn't enlighten her about his name, she continued coldly, and bitterly, 'I'm aware of what it means all right. If I could have found a job elsewhere, do you think I'd be sitting here?'

'What sort of work are you looking for? No,' he said sharply, as she opened her mouth to tell him, 'let me guess.'

Having no desire to be subject to his cool scrutiny again, it took her all her time to sit still as he studied her closely. 'A soft, seductive little voice, a rather charming, genteel little air, not exactly suggestive of poverty but hinting at something I can't exactly place . . .'

When he paused, frowning, she broke in, not wishing him to probe further, hoping to divert him. 'I'd rather remain a mystery, if you don't mind. Anyway,' she tried to smile lightly, 'women are supposed to be the mysterious sex.'

'Never to me.'

Because most women would chase after a man like this quite blatantly, she supposed, suppressing a little sigh, and knowing an odd urge to defy him. 'It's a good thing all men aren't cynics.'

'Be quiet,' he told her, yet with a hint of seriousness she found confusing as he continued studying her. 'You're obviously still in your teens.'

'Twenty.'

'I can hardly remember,' his mouth thinned wryly, with a twist of self mockery. 'At thirty-seven it doesn't pay to. So, you could be at university, where I believe I was at your age, but as you're not, you have to be doing something artistic, I think?'

'I'm a singer.' She was so astonished at his shrewdness that she parted with the information before she quite realised what she was saying.

If she had hoped he would be impressed she would have been disappointed. He looked faintly surprised but not enraptured.

'And can you sing?' he asked.

What a nerve! Her eyes sparkled angrily. 'Of course I can! At least,' she faltered, her brief burst of confidence no more than that, 'I may not be the best, but I manage to earn my living.'

'Why singing?'

She wished he would stop adding weight to each of his words, like a judge sentencing a criminal. 'I couldn't find anything else.'

'Did you bother to look?'

Now she was left in no doubt as to his disapproval, but what was it to him what she did? He was merely whiling away a boring hour and she was making the most of his protective company. Once in London they would never meet again. Granted, he was easy to talk to—in a way, but she couldn't tell him about her family. It would be both silly and senseless to involve them.

No amount of reasoning, however, would eliminate an almost compulsive desire to defend herself. 'I sang with a group in Manchester, night clubs mostly. Then one of the men,' she didn't tell him it was her brother, 'got married and went abroad to try his luck. He married an American, you see.'

'You were in love with this man?'

'Of course not!' she exclaimed, flushing hotly.

He viewed her scarlet cheeks cynically. 'The evidence points otherwise, I'm afraid. A whole group doesn't usually split up because one member leaves. He must have been replaceable, if not in your affections, with the band?'

'It was just one of those things,' she mumbled finding it impossible to explain that without Andrew's protection she had been wholly at the mercy of the group leader. Rick Portman had been in love with her and just waiting the first opportunity to get her on her own. If someone hadn't rescued her, the first night she had worked alone, she might have been scarred for life. Was she always going to need rescuing? she wondered bitterly, railing helplessly against her inadequate feminine strength.

The man was asking tersely, 'If you couldn't continue singing in Manchester, why didn't you just pack it in?'

'You mean—change my career?'

'Yes.'

The table top had no pattern on it or it might have helped. Such flat brownness was hardly inspiring. Again a preverse streak refused to let her confess how her ageing, doting parents lived in a dream world, refusing to accept that they had only a meagre pension to live on. Alana's father, never practical, had been dominated by his father, who had kept his son in luxury in exchange for his blind obedience. Alana's father had been retiring age when his father died penniless, leaving him bereft and without the income he had been used to. Andrew had done his best, but with only music in his blood his prospects, because he wasn't brilliant, had been limited. Not until Alana had insisted on joining him as a singer had their financial position improved. It had been a crazy, rather desperate idea, for she had been fresh from school, but the band had decided to give her a trial and she had been an instant success. Her voice wasn't strong, but people liked it, while men clamoured over her lovely young face and the seductive lines of her slender body. Between them, she and Andrew had managed to keep their parents in comparative comfort.

Then Andrew had met a girl from New York and in a few short weeks they had been married. He had promised to send money, but a month ago had written to say Tally was pregnant and suffering from some rare, heredity disease and all their spare cash was going on medical expenses. In despair, for her parents were in debt again, Alana had decided to try London, rather than continue looking hopelessly for work in Manchester, where every group she approached appeared to consist of friends of Rick Portman.

'I might have changed my occupation,' she found herself replying absently, as her companion stirred impatiently, 'but few other jobs pay enough.'

'Enough for what?'

She blinked at his tone. 'To live on,' she said bleakly. 'I've discovered one can't live without money and I—er—like to help my parents—occasionally.'

Any softness in his eyes disappeared as his manner changed. 'The usual excuse, I suppose. Why can't you be honest and admit you're after money solely for your own use? It's amazing how many youngsters still imagine the streets of London are paved with gold.'

'I'm scarcely a youngster,' she rejoined coldly, biting her lip against a more heated protest.

'That I am well aware of,' he retorted dryly.

Something in his voice startled her, bringing her glance to his face. As their eyes met the peculiar electric tension began dancing between them again, tightening the nerves in Alana's throat until she feared she might choke. If we were lovers, she thought irrationally, we wouldn't need to touch. To look at each other might be enough.

'And how,' he asked curtly, pinning her dazed eyes with his own narrowing ones, 'do you intend going about finding something in London? Don't you realise there are hundreds of girls looking for the kind of work you're after, all carried away by the thought of seeing their name in lights? The competition is cut-throat, and you do understand what it can involve?'

'At least everyone must stand the same chance!'

'Are you out of your tiny little mind?' His mouth curled with a sarcasm that made her flinch. 'More often it depends on how much a girl is prepared to give? Surely, in your career to date, you've found out that much?'

When she thought of Rick Portman her face coloured, but then she had always had Andrew as an effective buffer. He had protected her from all the bad things, although she hadn't been fully aware that it had been necessary until after he had gone.

'I'm not altogether naïve,' she retorted indignantly, 'but I think, like a lot of people, you tend to exaggerate the seamy side of entertainment. You forget this can apply to life in general. I know what I'm doing, nothing's going to happen to me.'

He treated this trite statement to the cynically raised eyebrow, he obviously believed it deserved. 'Well, your virtue, if you still have it, is no concern of mine. If you're prepared to sleep around . . .'

'I don't sleep around!' she interrupted tightly.

'Then it might be easier if you learnt to,' he taunted remorselessly. 'Is it any use suggesting you stay with me for a few weeks?'

'No use at all,' she replied furiously, her hand itching to slap his hard, handsome face. Yet, despite her anger, her heart was thumping and it was incredible, for all he maddened her, that she had a feeling she was merely postponing the inevitable.

'So,' he murmured, with an indifference she didn't find exactly flattering, 'how do you propose carving a name and fortune for yourself, now you've found the courage to leave home?'

'For a start,' she snapped, torn beyond endurance, 'I don't have to stay here and listen to your sarcasm!

Grateful though I am for your help, I'll find somewhere else to sit, if you don't want to move.'

Jumping to her feet as she delivered her speech with
a flourish, she paused aghast as her glance chanced to
fall on the carriage door. The two youths were there
again and as her eyes widened with dismay and her
voice trailed off in alarm, the man beside her turned to
see what was wrong. Fortunately, when they saw he
was still there, the boys fled.

The stranger shifted his gaze back to her, smiling
softly. 'Are you going to join them?'

'No,' she shuddered, sitting down again, appealing
to him, almost ready to agree to anything he might
demand. 'I'm sorry if I've been too hasty. I'd be very
grateful,' she added humbly, 'if you haven't anything
else to do, if you'd stay with me until we reach
London.'

'No trouble at all,' he answered smoothly, with an
irritating quirk of amusement. 'We can all be a little
hasty at times. You do realise, of course, that it might
be wiser if we left the station together. They could be
waiting. I don't suggest they're anything but harmless,
but bored youths will do anything for a little entertainment.'

'It's a risk I'll have to take.' Some instinct warned
her it was as imperative to escape this stranger as the
two lurking youths. 'I'll take a taxi.'

'Where to?' He looked hard at her anxious face.

She felt like telling him to mind his own business
and knew she mustn't. It would be rude, and she owed
him too much. 'I'll find a room. Maybe the taxi driver
will be able to help. If not—well, there must be information bureaus or something?'

'My God!' he exclaimed dryly, 'you are still wet
behind the ears! Don't you know a room of any kind is
about as easy to find in London as the gold I mentioned? Unless you know someone?'

'Well, I don't.' She had to sound careless, which was better than bursting into tears. It must be crazy, the situation she was in, having to sit here and be coolly insulted by a man she was too scared to leave.

'Listen,' he paused, with what might have been a grim flicker of self-mockery, 'I don't know why I should offer to help, but it won't do my conscience any good if I just go off and leave you on your own. You may have all the experience you boast of, but you still look too innocent for your own good.'

Alana did her best to ignore this. 'You mean you know where I can find a room?'

He replied slowly, 'I happen to know of a hotel where they run a nightclub, one of the best in London, I may add, and they're always on the lookout for new talent.'

She was incredulous. 'I find it difficult to believe . . .'

'I can't make you believe,' he looked as if he didn't really care whether she did or not, 'but you must have thought you had a chance, otherwise why did you bother to come to London? Anyway,' before she could reply, 'I'm not guaranteeing you a job, that's up to you, but if you like I'll give you a note to take to Milo Sachs, who runs the show at the Remax, and if he likes the look of you he might give you an audition.'

Alana swallowed with difficulty. 'Is—is Mr Sachs a friend of yours?'

'I suppose so.'

'You—you aren't one of his talent spotters?' She could have sworn his mouth twitched and glanced at him suspiciously. 'Well, are you?'

'Not officially, shall we say,' his face was quite sober so she must have imagined his amusement, 'just this once, in your case.'

Alana didn't know what to think. Could she afford to be suspicious? She had heard of the Remax Hotel—

who hadn't? It must be world-famous, on par with the Ritz and the Savoy. Surely they wouldn't even consider a young and unknown singer?

'Do you work there, too?' she asked suddenly.

He might have been expecting a query of this kind, for he answered immediately. 'Occasionally, when they're short-staffed.'

'Oh, I see.' She wasn't sure that she did, but it seemed to explain the situation, if only vaguely. 'I hope you don't think I'm being too curious,' she rushed on in confusion, 'but—well, I mean, if I did get taken on I should want to thank you.'

'And what if I demanded more than you were prepared to give?' he asked dryly. As she stared at him aghast, he ignored her mutinous little gasp. 'Calm down, child. You can repay me by putting a good performance, otherwise Milo will think I've taken leave of my senses.'

That would be the day, she thought wryly, unable to remember meeting a man who seemed less likely to be swayed by his emotions. With a strange conviction that she must be dreaming, she watched as he took a small notepad from his pocket and scribbled something on it. Tearing out the sheet, he folded it in two before addressing it to Milo Sachs. Then he gave it to her.

'Who do I say sent me?' Alana handled the note as if it was red-hot in her hands.

'It's all there,' he replied. 'Open it and see.'

Reluctantly, for he seemed to have the knack of angering her, she did so. Guy Mason? She had never heard of anyone called Guy Mason—and there were only two words. 'It wasn't a note,' she pointed out, bewildered.

'It will be enough,' he said, with a hint of the arrogance she had noted previously. 'He'll know what it's about.'

'I hope so.'

'Now,' he murmured, dismissing her worried expression as of no consequence, 'we're arriving at Euston. If you come with me I'll fix you up with a room for the night.'

Alana was so busy listening to him she failed to realise they had reached London. Decidedly flustered, both by this and his second surprising offer, she scrambled breathlessly to her feet. 'No, please, Mr Mason. You've done enough.'

'I never believe,' he assured her coolly, 'in leaving a job half done.' His glance going over her smoothly, he reached for her case. 'You haven't told me your name?'

'Alana Hurst,' she said quickly, thinking wistfully that if she had been good at her job and famous, he wouldn't have needed to ask. As he nodded a brief acknowledgement, she viewed his appropriation of her suitcase doubtfully. 'You said there are no rooms available.'

'I'm not suggesting you share with me, not yet, but I can get you in somewhere.'

She distrusted the ironic glint in his eyes and tried to tell herself she wasn't wholly reliant on him. She might never have met him and would somehow have managed on her own. The trouble was that, having met him, she found herself clinging almost desperately to his strength. 'I—I can't afford a lot,' she stammered, trying anxiously to reinstate her independence.

'Don't worry,' Guy Mason said, guiding her from the now stationary train and through the barrier, 'You can repay me if Milo likes you. If you're good and he does, you'll soon be able to afford something much more luxurious than I'm supplying tonight. If not, then there are other ways, but we needn't consider them for the moment.'

'Oh, but——' She paused abruptly, having been going to say that if she did begin earning a salary she must send what she could spare home. The likelihood of Mr Sachs taking her on, however, was so remote as to make arguing over such an issue seem a futile exercise. There must be other ways, as Mr Mason hinted, but he might have to wait a long time, and she didn't want to be in anyone's debt. Wasn't it bad enough trying to cope with the debts of others?

Her alarm grew as he dismissed her muddled protests firmly and bundled her into a waiting taxi. Off the train, he appeared more authoritative than ever, and this, combined with his tall, well built body, seemed to remove any chance she had of making a stand against him. As they drove across London he relaxed back in his seat and made no further attempts to engage her in conversation.

She must be mad, she thought drearily, closing her eyes as he stared calmly at her beautiful profile. She wished he would stop considering her as a potential buyer might consider an intriguing painting. She recognised the symptoms, for she was an ardent haunter of art galleries herself. In his manner was the slightest hint of speculation, of increasing satisfaction, mixing with a deepening certainty that he had found a masterpiece. Of course he would be thinking of his friend Milo's gratitude if she turned out to be a winner. Probably Mr Sachs was very generous to those who served his interests well.

Guy Mason didn't interrupt her unhappy thoughts and silence reigned until they drew up outside a large but shabby house in a quiet street.

'Come with me,' he commanded, instructing the taxi to wait.

A woman opened the door when he rang the bell, an elderly woman, walking with a stick. 'Why, good gracious!' she exclaimed, her eyes round with surprise as she saw who was there. 'You haven't been here for a long time, Mr Guy.'

'I know, Joan,' he smiled, 'I've been busy. You know how it is.'

'I expect you're still struggling as hard as ever to make a living?' the woman smiled.

As Guy Mason grinned back, Alana frowned, immediately thinking of the waiting taxi. The fare must be mounting up, and if Mr Mason wasn't very affluent he mightn't be able to pay it.

She was trying to think of a tactful way of calling his attention to this when she heard him saying. 'Your spare room, Joan? This young lady,' he drew Alana forward, introducing her briefly, 'has nowhere to go. Could she have it?'

Joan, whom he had introduced as Mrs Brice, hesitated, peering at Alana uncertainly. 'I wasn't going to let it again, you know.'

'Just this once?' he coaxed.

Hating his wheedling tone, and that she was the cause of it, Alana said quickly that she could easily look for something else.

'No, you can't,' he silenced her with a glance quite different from the warmer one he had bestowed on Mrs Brice. 'Come on, Joan,' he smiled at her again, 'it'll only be for one night, two at the most.'

Joan sighed but nodded. 'I could never say no to you, Mr Guy. That's always been my trouble.'

'Get along with you,' he laughed, 'and remember, no talking. Miss Hurst needs her beauty sleep.'

Why did Alana feel the bit about no talking had nothing to do with whether she slept or not? But before she could puzzle it out he had turned to go.

'I wish you luck, Miss Hurst,' he said dryly, after saying goodbye to Joan.

'Don't be so long in coming back,' Joan called.

'I won't,' he promised.

Alana was still feeling dazed as she followed Mrs Brice into the house after picking up her case. As they

went upstairs she almost pinched herself to make sure
she wasn't dreaming. It could, of course, be a night-
mare she was having. How did she know she could
trust either Guy Mason or this woman? Mrs Brice
looked homely and honest, but this might not be true.

The room she was shown to was pleasant and had a
small kitchen attached, complete with a cooker and
fridge.

'It's really a flat,' Mrs Brice explained. 'I used to let
it regularly, but the last people I had weren't satisfactory and, as I was saying before, I decided not to let it
again. However, I'd do anything to oblige Mr Guy.'

'It's very kind of you,' Alana hesitated. 'I'd hate to
feel I was being a nuisance, though. Do you often have
to oblige Mr Mason?'

'Mr who . . .? Oh, I see.' For a moment Mrs Brice
looked confused. 'No, this is actually the first time
he's ever asked me to have anyone specially.'

With a sigh Alana dropped her suitcase by the bed.
She would liked to have gone on asking questions about
Guy Mason, but she guessed Mrs Brice mightn't be
prepared to divulge anything more. Ruefully she
smiled and was surprised to find Mrs Brice watching
her, her eyes softening as she regarded Alana's pale
young face.

'I was just about to have my supper,' she said, 'when
the doorbell rang. Perhaps you'd like to join me, if you
haven't already eaten? It's only ham and salad, but
there's plenty.'

When Alana nodded gratefully, she stood aside with
a motherly smile to let her go down the stairs first.

CHAPTER TWO

AFTER lunch next day Alana made her way rather apprehensively towards the Remax. She had been going to go earlier, but Mrs Brice, who appeared to know about such things, advised her to wait.

'It's highly unlikely Mr Sachs gets to bed before dawn, love,' she said at breakfast. 'You might only be wasting your time.'

Mrs Brice was kind and though inclined to be talkative, Alana soon found, as she had suspected the night before, that she wasn't prepared to talk about Mr Mason. She had once cooked for his mother, this was all she would say, and Alana wasn't able to bring herself to ask anything more. That he had been kind didn't automatically give her the right to be over-curious about him.

Mrs Brice was elderly but still quite active. She heated some soup for their supper and made a huge pot of tea to go with the ham and salad. This morning she had insisted on Alana joining her for breakfast as well and wouldn't take the five pounds Alana offered.

'No, I'm not offended, love,' she smiled, when Alana feared she might be. 'It will be a sad day when I can't give someone a cup of tea, but Mr Guy will settle with me, then you can see him.'

She had told Alana the best place in the district to buy provisions and Alana had spent what was left of the morning stocking up with a few modest supplies, enough to keep her going until the following day when she was determined to make more permanent arrangements. Despite Mrs Brice's protests, she bought her a chicken and some sherry which appeared to delight the old lady very much.

The weather was cold, but following Mrs Brice's directions she had little trouble in finding the Remax. The hotel, in the West End, caused her to draw a quick breath. Outside, the façade was restrained but imposing, while inside it was quietly but definitely luxurious. And, if she hadn't already known, Alana would only have needed a glimpse at the clientele to have guessed what grade it was in.

Very conscious of her shabby, belted raincoat, she asked at the reception desk where she could find Mr Sachs and was rewarded with a haughty glance from one of the elegant young ladies.

'Have you an appointment? Does he know you're coming?'

'Not exactly,' Alana stammered.

'I'm afraid he doesn't see casual callers,' she was told politely.

'I—I have a note.' Nervously Alana delved deep in her handbag, managing by sheer luck to extract it immediately.

She thrust it at the girl, who looked at it dubiously before reluctantly beckoning a bellboy. 'Here, James,' she said in bored tones, 'you can take this to Mr Sachs and see if there's any answer.'

Anxiously, while the girl wandered off to attend to someone else, Alana watched for the boy's return. When he did he signalled for her to follow him at once.

'Come this way,' he requested, looking slightly agitated.

Obviously Mr Sachs wasn't in the best of moods, and Alana's heart sank. Oh, well, she thought, trying to be philosophical, it was all good experience and she was lucky to have even got as far as this. She mustn't allow one setback to discourage her. There were other places.

The decor was magnificent. She shuddered to think what the carpets alone must have cost. As she followed James her feet literally sank into them and she realised wistfully that she would find few places in the same class as the Remax. The people who owned it must be millionaires!

Mr Sachs's dressing room was small and shabby by comparison, but she didn't take much notice. As her glance settled on its occupant she trembled with nervousness. He was of medium height, a youngish man, with a slightly foreign look about him. The bellboy departed, closing the door behind him. Alana found herself wishing he had stayed.

'Tell me, darling,' Mr Sachs scarcely raised his head from the newspaper he was reading, 'what experience do you have?'

Briefly she told him, then asked, 'The man I met on the train, the one who gave me this introduction—I hope he wasn't—well, overstepping his authority?'

Mr Sachs dropped his newspaper with a sarcastic grin. 'Guy has a habit of poking his nose in where it isn't wanted, but he doesn't expect us to appreciate it every time.'

What a peculiar thing to say! Alana felt bewildered. 'He gave the impression that he was used to being obeyed,' she faltered, 'but I'd rather be accepted on my own merit. I mean, I wouldn't want him to influence your judgment.'

'No?' His mouth quirked again, and she wondered what was amusing him. Something was, she felt sure. His next statement was so ambiguous she was left feeling more confused than ever. 'Let's see whether you can really sing, then we'll begin to argue about whether you can stay or not.'

'Thank you,' she murmured, her eyes wide and innocent, very blue.

He glanced at her again, his eyes lingering curiously.

He said quickly, as if seeking an excuse for staring at her, 'You'd better take that raincoat off. It's not all that important to see what's underneath at this stage, but I like to get the general impression.'

'Yes, Mr Sachs.' She began fumbling with the belt with trembling fingers. He made her feel nervous, not in the same way as Guy Mason did, but he had the same habit of regarding her closely.

'Call me Milo,' he said, getting slowly to his feet.

There was a small band playing, obviously practising, in a huge, slightly shrouded room. As they entered there was a sudden silence while Milo introduced her casually. He asked her to name her favourite tune and when she did he told the band to play it. Then, after waiting a minute or two until she relaxed, he signalled for her to start singing.

A little later Milo said—and she couldn't help being aware of the faint surprise in his voice, 'I think, darling, with a little polishing up you might do. Come back to the office with me and we'll talk.'

She obeyed, smiling tentatively at the men who sat with their various instruments, listening with interest. She felt grateful for the co-operation they had given her. They might almost have sensed her whole future was at stake, and could depend on her performance that afternoon.

In his office, Milo rang for coffee and while they waited asked her several questions which she tried to answer to the best of her ability.

When the coffee arrived and they were drinking it, he said thoughtfully, 'You need practice, Alana, but you have a certain something which I like. Your voice may never launch a thousand ships, but it's nice, and surprisingly sexy. I say surprisingly sexy because you have such an air of innocence about you.' As Alana winced, he grinned and went on, 'You'll have to be dressed up, of course, and your hair and face need seeing to. Your hair,' his eyes went closely over it, 'is terrific. I've never seen such a blonde mane. It could be outstanding with the right treatment, and if you leave everything to me, I'll see that you get it.'

With his coffee cup in his hand he walked around her looking almost jubilant. 'Don't take any notice of me,' he laughed, as she blinked in confusion, 'I always get slightly carried away by something that turns out better than I thought it would be.'

Alana stood dazed as he added something about life still holding a few pleasant surprises. Half of what he said went over her head. She only wished he would ask her to sit down. Having been standing since she first arrived, she now felt ready to drop. Milo seemed to like her, though, and she'd never thought it would be so easy to find work. It had certainly been a stroke of good luck, meeting Guy Mason on the train. She knew of some really good singers who had been out of work for months.

'Does this mean you'll take me on?' she dared ask at last.

'Yes, Miss Hurst, it does,' he smiled. 'At least, we'll give you a trial run, but I can almost guarantee it. There shouldn't be any problems. Trust Guy to pick a winner!' he chuckled. 'I guess that's half the secret of his . . .'

As he stopped abruptly, Alana wondered why he looked so embarrassed. 'Yes?' she prompted.

'Nothing,' he muttered, adopting the role of a stern employer. 'We'll forget about him, we have more important things to discuss. You're still very green, even if you look good and can sing.'

Why did she feel he knew something she didn't? He was being as secretive about Guy Mason as Mrs Brice had been, and she was sure it wasn't just a case of loyal friendship. Yet why should she want to know more about a man whose every glance had been like a baptism of fire? If she was never to see him again it would suit her fine!

Milo eventually did ask her to sit down and she sank gratefully into the chair at the other side of his desk. Then, just as he reached for a pad, the telephone rang. 'Yes?' he snapped. 'Okay, okay!' He slammed the receiver down again, obviously not pleased by the interruption. 'I have to see somebody,' he said, rising to his feet, 'but stay where you are, I won't be long.'

After he had gone Alana tried to relax and to really take in the incredible fact that she had found employment! She was just beginning to grasp her extreme good fortune when the door opened and Guy Mason walked in.

'Oh!' she murmured as her eyes immediately locked with his. The effect was alarming, as tiny flames at the back of his scorched her. She could feel them licking right down to her toes and back again. As her hands helplessly clutched her devastated stomach, his piercing glance relaxed for a moment, but only to move to her unsteady lips. Incredulously she felt the skin prickle as if he had kissed her.

With an effort she swallowed another gasp and asked quickly, 'Are you sure you should be here?'

He was still wearing jeans but had changed his black shirt. His casual attire caused Alana to wonder what he did. He gave no hint, however, as to his exact occupation and ignored what she said. 'I came to see how you got on. Any luck?'

She found the tall, leashed strength of his body nearly as hard to take as his eyes and averted her glance. 'I—I think so. Milo has been called away, but he seems to think I'll do.'

'I thought he might.'

Startled by his tone, her eyes flew back to his. 'You don't sound very approving?'

With a cynical twist of his lips, he walked over to a picture hanging on the wall. It was a painting of a beautiful dancer wearing a gown which was practically non-existent. 'Does this sort of thing appeal to you?' he asked.

Alana hadn't noticed the painting, she hadn't really had time. 'No, of course not,' she exclaimed, her cheeks scarlet as she saw his glance resting coolly on the dancer's almost naked breasts.

'For someone of your profession you seem astonishingly innocent,' he murmured tersely. 'Are you?'

'Am I what?' she floundered, thinking that if she ever heard the word again she would scream.

'Innocent, damn you!'

Shocked by his sudden harshness, she was stung to anger. He might have helped her get work, but this didn't give him the right to insult her, which he seemed to have been doing on and off since they met. And that hadn't been twenty-four hours ago!

'I may sing, but I don't sleep around, which I believe I told you last night,' she retorted furiously.

'Perhaps I'm just making sure,' he said.

'Well, you can be,' she cried.

'You realise,' he snapped, as though not yet satisfied, 'if you work here Milo might expect you to wear almost as little as the girl in this picture?'

'I'd refuse to be indecent!' She lifted her chin as he walked back to her.

'Some dresses might be indecent without your being aware of it. Milo's very good when it comes to getting his own way.'

'If you feel so bad about it, I don't know why you gave me this address in the first place.'

Their eyes sparkling coldly, they surveyed each other. Alana was conscious of his fury, although she could find no reason for it. Then the anger faded and between them seemed to lie a touch of madness. He came nearer, so she could feel his breath on her averted cheek and her nerves began tightening until she could have screamed wildly. She wanted to protest fiercely against something crazy that seemed to be happening to her, but his glittering glance was rendering her speechless.

His voice thickening slightly, he placed his hands on her shoulders. 'Maybe I do regret sending you here, but before Milo returns I want to ask you to have dinner with me this evening.'

How could he ask her to go out with him after speaking to her as he had been doing? Or was he merely looking for another chance to torment her? 'Would I enjoy myself?' she enquired bitterly.

'Of course.'

'You're very sure of yourself,' she commented sharply.

'No,' his hands moved over her sweater to the base of her throat, his thumbs tilting up her chin, 'I know what I want, which isn't quite the same thing.'

Something in his voice made her feel threatened, but it was his touch which sent a shiver rippling down her spine. 'You don't know what I want, though,' she replied breathlessly.

'I can feel your heart beating,' he taunted, putting a finger on its pulse. 'It's betraying you.'

His insolence was beyond belief! Angrily Alana jerked away from him. It was anger, she was convinced, that made her tremble.

'I'd have to ask Mr Sachs first,' she mumbled, scarcely realising she had given in. 'He might be expecting me to work this evening.'

'No, Alana, he won't be. The weekend, maybe, but not tonight. You can't just walk into a place like this straight from the provinces. You have to be prepared for the part.'

'How do you know?'

'It's standard procedure, my dear. I've seen it happen before.'

He would have, if he worked here—she'd forgotten about that. 'I don't like you,' she said, trying to believe it, 'but I suppose I can't refuse to have dinner with you, seeing how I owe you so much.'

'You mightn't be so sure you owe me anything in a few weeks' time,' Guy Mason answered cryptically, his eyes narrowing on her face.

Uneasily she stirred, not wishing to feel that the future could be anything but rosy for her now. 'Hadn't you better get back to whatever you're doing?' she suggested quickly. 'I wouldn't like to be responsible for you losing your job.'

'Oh, there's no fear of that,' he quipped dryly.

Her glance was puzzled. 'You must have a very tolerant boss. Is it a woman?' she asked, suddenly suspicious.

'Not yet,' his voice was even drier, 'but one day it might be.'

Women held all sorts of good positions and he obviously resented it. Alana did have a sneaking sympathy with him, for she couldn't see him in a subservient role, he was so arrogant. 'Perhaps you should try a little harder to get to the top yourself,' she said sweetly.

'It's an idea,' he agreed lightly. 'So I'll pick you up around seven?'

'I hope I'll be back,' she frowned, suddenly remembering. 'I was going to spend the rest of the afternoon looking for another room.'

Guy Mason paused on his way to the door, frowning as well. 'What's wrong with the one you've got?'

'Nothing,' she confessed honestly. 'It's very nice, but Mrs Brice is elderly and I feel I'm imposing on her.'

'Did she say so?'

'No . . .'

'Then I shouldn't worry about looking for something else. Stay where you are for the time being. Once Milo decides you'll do and you sign a contract with us—with the hotel, I mean, you'll be moving in here.'

Things were happening too quickly, she wasn't sure she could take it all in. 'I don't know if I would like that,' she faltered. 'It might not be wise.'

'You'll soon change your mind when you see what I—what Milo has lined up for you,' he said cynically. 'I'd be willing to bet my last cent you won't be able to resist it.'

Before she could express the indignation she felt at having her affairs arranged in this fashion, Milo returned and she was forced to bite her lip. She wasn't vindictive and she feared Guy Mason would get into trouble if Milo knew he'd been telling her things she wasn't supposed to know about until later.

'Hello, Guy,' said Milo, as the other man stood aside with a brief nod to let him pass. Dropping a file impatiently on his desk, Milo glanced from one to the other. 'You two been renewing your acquaintance?'

'In a way,' Guy Mason drawled. 'I came along to see what you think of her.'

Milo pursed his lips while his eyebrows shot up as he lifted his shoulders. 'She was born yesterday, but she'll do—or she will, when I'm finished with her.'

For a moment Alana was startled by a glimpse of rage she imagined she saw in Guy's face. Then the hardness relaxed and he shrugged. 'Soft-pedal a bit, Milo, won't you? She's not unattractive as she is.'

How dared they talk about her as if she wasn't here? Alana's hands clenched angrily. Then she saw that Milo was frowning as well as herself and Guy Mason had disappeared.

'I—I hope you don't think I was encouraging him,' she stammered.

Something like amusement twisted Milo's mouth

and she suspected he was laughing at her. Of course it would amuse him to hear it suggested that Guy Mason could be encouraged by a girl of her age—unless he was willing.

If Milo was amused it didn't last long. 'You don't understand the half of it, darling,' he muttered. 'This could lead to complications. Guy doesn't know the meaning of encouragement. He either likes a girl or he doesn't. If he does she doesn't stand a chance. He takes her out until he tires of her, then she's usually heart-broken and her work suffers, and I don't want this happening to you.'

'Does he have many girl-friends?' she asked in a small voice, wondering why she felt so depressed.

'No,' Milo sounded slightly thoughtful. 'I'm not saying he's any monk, but it's a few years since I've seen him with anyone regularly. That's why I'm sus-picious of his sudden interest in you. Apart from any-thing else, it wouldn't be convenient.'

'I don't think Mr Mason would be seriously inter-ested in a girl like me,' Alana said carefully, washed by yet another mysterious wave of depression. 'But, just supposing he was, how would it not be convenient?'

'When I take a girl on I like her to be dedicated,' Milo grunted, 'to her singing, dancing, or whatever,' he threw up his hands. 'If she needs a lover I might allow it, as long as it's someone who won't upset what she's doing.'

'And you believe Mr Mason could do that?'

'Mr Mason is an entirely different matter.'

Milo was hedging. Alana didn't understand what he was on about and she didn't think he had any intention of explaining. It could be that Guy Mason knew something about Milo, or had some kind of hold over him which put Milo slightly in his power.

'If Mr Mason works here,' she asked, trying to speak carelessly, 'what does he do?'

'Oh, this and that,' Milo replied vaguely. 'He usually goes around the group—of hotels, that is, helping out, wherever he's needed most.'

'He sounds like an odd job man,' she retorted dryly, thinking with irritation that as no one seemed prepared to tell her she wouldn't ask again.

Milo, apparently as willing to drop the subject, began talking about her contract. The terms he mentioned were good, the money better than anything had she had before.

'When do I start?' she asked.

'Next week,' he said, confirming what Guy Mason had told her. 'But we have a lot to do before then.'

Alana glanced at him uncertainly, the terrible worry at the back of her mind refusing to remain there. 'I don't suppose you could possibly let me have an—an advance?'

'Advance?' His eyes narrowed as if he was surprised to hear such a request coming from her. 'How much?'

She flushed, never dreaming it would be so hard, 'I'd be grateful if you could let me have, say, five hundred pounds?'

'Five hundred!' he frowned, staring at her closely. 'Are you in debt, or is it something you want to buy?'

Which would sound better? Or, rather, which would sound worse? If she said it was for something she wanted to buy, it mightn't sound so bad, but he could easily tell her to forget it. Deciding on the truth, she murmured dully. 'It's to pay off a debt.'

'I see . . .' he pondered. 'Well, it should be possible, but my middle name isn't Father Christmas. I'll have to have a word with management.'

'It will be confidential?' She wondered how she had the nerve to ask?

'Naturally,' he assured her with a sigh.

Alana wished she could have told him the money was for her parents, but as usual she remained silent,

unconsciously defending them. It wasn't their fault
they couldn't cope and it hurt that no one but she and
Andrew had any sympathy for them. The last close
friends of theirs, whom Alana had approached con-
cerning their plight, had been so withering in their
comments that she had vowed never to mention it
again. Five hundred should tide them over, and she
hoped desperately that Milo would succeed in getting
it for her.

Mrs Brice was happy about Alana's new job and
agreeable to her keeping the room. Alana didn't ask, it
was Mrs Brice who suggested it.

'I'm not going to pretend I'm lonely or that I need
the money,' she said, 'but you're a nice young girl and
I feel you might be safer with me.'

'Mr Sachs would like me to live at the hotel,' Alana
explained, 'but I'd rather live here. I'm not sure if I'll
be allowed a say in the matter, but if I can choose, I'll
stay with you.'

They shared a pot of tea and the cake Alana had
purchased earlier while she told Mrs Brice about her
audition and how nice everyone had been. Then she
remembered she was going out to dinner and her
clothes were still unpacked, which meant she would
have to press a dress before it was fit to wear.

There was no comment when she said she was going
out with Guy Mason, but forewarned, Alana didn't
expect any. She only mentioned it out of courtesy,
because Mrs Brice had been kind and she was a friend
of Guy Mason's.

When she came down ready, at seven prompt, she
was surprised to find him sitting talking to Mrs Brice
in the kitchen. She hadn't heard the doorbell.

'Mr Guy came early,' Mrs Brice smiled. 'And you
won't hear the bell upstairs, dear, the connection's
broken. I wasn't going to get it fixed, but as you might
be staying . . .'

'She won't be,' Guy said curtly, 'so don't bother. She'll be at the hotel.'

Alana felt furious as they left, as he put her in the waiting taxi. 'How can you be so sure I'll be at the hotel?' she asked. 'Nothing's been decided.'

'I heard before I left,' he replied, sitting so near she could feel his thigh pressing against her. 'You're to go there at the weekend.'

'I can always refuse,' she retorted, with more confidence than she felt.

He turned to stare at her coldly as the taxi drove away and she wondered why he should be so contemptuous. During the brief period she had known him he had often looked disapproving, but never more so than now.

'I think you're in no position to do other than what you're told to do,' he said dryly.

'Whatever do you mean?' Her eyes widened apprehensively as she feared Milo might have let something slip about the money she had asked for.

'Is it necessary to explain?' He didn't mention the money at all. 'You wouldn't find it as easy to find another job. Milo happens to like your voice, but it might not appeal to everyone. You were lucky. You could try a dozen places and be turned away.'

It was true, of course. She nodded helplessly.

'And,' he continued relentlessly, 'if you were allowed to stay with Mrs Brice, have you ever considered the other aspects? You leave the club at say two or three in the morning and some man is waiting to molest you.'

'It's unlikely,' she protested.

'But not unknown,' he assured her grimly, 'and there are other pitfalls apart from the human ones. Have you ever given a thought to taxi fares and the cost of running a flat? At the Remax everything would be on the house.'

Alana frowned. He was right, she hadn't thought of this. It must certainly make a difference, living in, as it was called. Wouldn't she be foolish to refuse free board and lodgings, especially if it meant she would have more money to send home?

'It makes sense,' she agreed wistfully, 'I've always lived with my parents and I suppose I was looking forward to being independent.' With a sigh, she lay back in her seat and tried to stop thinking of her parents as the taxi sped through the brightly lit streets. 'Do you live at the hotel?' she asked, as the familiar tension began mounting between them again and seemed suddenly unbearable.

'When I'm there,' he replied shortly, 'it's convenient.'

'Milo says you travel around.'

'Milo talks too much.'

Alana gave him an anxious look. 'He doesn't strike me as being a gossip. I think he's very nice. I'm really looking forward to working with him.'

'Just as long as you concentrate on your work.' His mouth tightened. 'I believe Sachs has a fiancée tucked away somewhere.'

'You have a one-track mind, don't you,' she flared, 'where I'm concerned. How many times do I have to tell you I'm not interested in that kind of thing!'

'Aren't you?' His voice was cynical.

He might as well have called her a liar and been done with it! 'I have my career to think of,' she said coldly.

'Of course,' he murmured, so sarcastically she could have hit him.

She didn't care for the mood he was in. Last night he had been cold and mocking, but this evening his coldness was of a different kind. It bewildered her. Making a great effort, she changed the subject, rather than continue arguing with him. 'Where are you taking me?'

'To the most expensive place I can find,' he answered coolly. 'A girl like you always demands the best. Give her anything else and a man doesn't have a hope of seeing her again.'

'If you'd stop this taxi I'd like to get out!' she said between her teeth.

'Now what have I said?' He pretended injured innocence.

Hating him, she retorted, 'You insinuated I would go to the highest bidder.'

'And you wouldn't?' His mouth twisted as he studied her furious indignation. Suddenly he grasped her wrist, his hand tight and hurting on the soft skin. 'All right, maybe I am being a bit hard on you and I'm willing to apologise, but if you're trying to fool me it's you who's going to be sorry.'

'I'm not trying to fool you.' No amount of tugging could release her wrist and she was startled at the way his touch affected her breathing. 'At the same time,' she gasped, 'I think this conversation's more than ridiculous. You don't own me!'

'Not quite yet,' he murmured mockingly.

Oh, what was the use! She watched helplessly as he lifted her wrist to his mouth and began softly kissing the sore skin. By the time he finished and laid her hand back in her lap, she was incapable of summoning up further anger. She could still feel the thrill which swept through her whole body at his brief caress.

All the fight knocked out of her, she said humbly, 'I'd rather you didn't spend a lot of money on me, honestly. I'd be quite happy with a snack at a sandwich bar or somewhere like that.'

'Well, I wouldn't.'

Hastily Alana decided to drop the issue and leave it to him. If his mother employed cooks, or had employed them, it seemed likely he was from a fairly wealthy family. Or a family that had been wealthy. This evening, dressed in a fine three-piece suit and white shirt, he was both handsome and distinguished. However humble his present circumstances, he still retained an air of cool, dark arrogance. And, however mad he made her, she wouldn't be guilty of taking away his pride. Perhaps he hadn't much left to be proud about, but even so, she must leave him the last remnants. Her own circumstances weren't anything to boast of, she was ready to admit. She and Guy probably had a lot more in common than they realised.

But as she glanced at him quickly, the conciliatory smile died on her lips as she was again made aware of something potent moving between them. Uneasily, as her heart increased its beating, she tried to move away from him. Whatever it was she must forget it. Her new job might be difficult enough without complications of another kind.

As she huddled in the corner, his gaze mocked her. 'Falling out of the window couldn't be less dangerous than staying near me. If I wanted to make love to you— when I do,' he amended coolly, 'it won't be in a taxi.'

Cheeks flaming, anger returning, Alana clutched tightly on her handbag. 'I owe you a lot, but my gratitude doesn't extend as far as that. If you're under the impression that it does, then you're wasting your time!'

His mouth tightened. 'I'd be the last to take advantage of your questionable gratitude and you might be wiser to be careful of what you say. There's something between us, as you're well aware, call it libido or whatever you like. I'm not very sure myself, yet. But this I do know. One day you'll want me as much as I maybe want you—and say much more, and you might have to beg.'

What could be the use of reiterating all she had said before about not being that kind of a girl? 'Don't worry,' her voice was as terse as his, 'I don't imagine instant attraction ever lasts.'

'It's certainly better not to plan the rest of one's life around it,' he said cynically, 'but at the same time it doesn't do to ignore these things altogether.'

'I'd rather wait and fall in love for keeps,' she declared fiercely. 'I don't want an affair.'

'Marriage can involve a lot more.'

'It's possible,' she tried to keep her voice steady, 'but it has a sense of permanency about it.'

'What about the prodigious number of divorces?' he came back.

'Perhaps if people all start out as doubtful as you it's no wonder,' she retorted heatedly. 'You have to give any kind of relationship a chance.'

Tongue in cheek, he asked, 'As you're such an expert, what would you say would be the best way for a man to form a satisfactory relationship with a night club singer, if he doesn't want to marry her?'

Somehow that hurt, although she tried to ignore it. 'I don't have to answer that,' she said coldly, relieved to find the taxi drawing up outside the dimly lit doors of a restaurant.

CHAPTER THREE

THE restaurant which Guy Mason took her to might not have been the most expensive in London, but Alana thought it must be one of the most exclusive. She wasn't very familiar with London. When she had been here with her parents they had stayed at the Cumberland and visited Harrods and Hyde Park and, when she was small, the Zoo. When she was older they had taken her to the theatre and she had swopped the museums for art galleries, but that was all. Most of the city still remained a mystery and she hoped, during the following weeks, to be able to get to know it better.

They had a drink at the bar and carried second ones to their table, where they studied the menu and ordered. Alana wasn't familiar with half the dishes offered and had to rely on Guy's advice. As he was something of an expert, the meal proved a veritable feast, which she enjoyed very much. Or would have done if it hadn't been for the persistent niggle at the back of her mind regarding the cost.

'Stop worrying!' he taunted, well aware of what lay behind her anxious frown when he suggested she might enjoy the out-of-season strawberries. 'I'm feeling extravagant tonight and I'm not going to ask you to pay your share.'

'You can laugh,' she retorted, 'but I couldn't afford this kind of thing.'

'What do you spend your money on?' His eyes narrowed as they went over the dress she was wearing, judging its value exactly.

It was flattering but inexpensive. Alana felt her cheeks growing hot. She never had much to spend on clothes as she gave her parents any salary she earned and only received pocket money back. It was almost impossible to save enough to buy anything decent. The dress she wore tonight was a sale reduction and better than most which she owned, but compared with what the women at the other tables were wearing, she realised it didn't stand a chance.

'I don't spend it on pricey restaurants, anyway,' she muttered defensively. 'In a place like this I imagine every breath we take will be charged for.'

Guy wouldn't allow her to avoid answering his question so easily. And the glint in his eyes assured her he knew exactly what she was doing. 'I can guess the price of your dress, and you're wearing no jewellery.'

He looked faintly puzzled and she wondered why. 'If I'd worn all the jewellery I possess,' she laughed, thinking it safer to treat the subject lightly, 'I might not have been able to get in the taxi.'

'You mean you don't have any,' he said flatly.

She could see no point in making an issue of it. 'Maybe I will have,' she shrugged, 'when I start working at the Remax. I might even attract a wealthy customer.'

'Do you plan to?' he snapped, appearing far from amused by what she had intended as a joke.

'I suppose I shall have to concentrate on my singing. Work first and pleasure afterwards,' she quipped, wondering how she had managed to annoy him.

She had refused wine with her meal, having had two drinks already and knowing her limits. As she refused again, she watched as he refilled his own glass impatiently. It didn't do to have anything but a clear head with Guy Mason. When he looked at her she felt disorientated enough without the added stimulation of wine. Her gaze fell to his watch, which she could have sworn was real gold, and his beautiful white cuffs. There was a slight coating of dark hair on the backs of his strong but extremely well kept hands. Curiosity overcame her.

'What exactly do you do?' she enquired.

As though aware he couldn't put her off for ever, he answered shortly, 'I assist management, a sort of advisory position.'

'You—do?' Her eyes widened with surprise.

'You didn't think I washed dishes, did you?'

'No,' she smiled, unable somehow to see him in a large apron, up to his elbows in soapsuds. 'How do you assist management, though?'

His voice was so casual she dismissed the impression that he was choosing his words. 'Large establishments, like the Remax, have all kinds of problems. Occasionally they have to call in someone to sort them out.'

That would account for his travelling around.

'So,' he said, sardonically, 'if your curiosity as well as your appetite is satisfied, Miss Hurst, I'll settle the bill and we'll get out of here.'

Outside the air was cool and he flagged down another taxi. The evening was over, he would take her back to Mrs Brice. Alana felt her spirits droop.

'Thank you for a pleasant evening,' she said.

'Wait until it's finished.' His dark brows rose.

'Isn't it?' she heard herself asking ingenuously.

'No. We're going to a night club, a London one, so you can see what goes on.'

'Oh, I don't think——' she began.

'I wish you wouldn't,' he cut in dryly. 'It would make a nice change.'

Refuse—be more emphatic, her common sense warned, while her heart beat out a different message. Go with him, it urged, but she was wary of his strong attraction. What could a sophisticated men like Guy Mason want with a girl like herself? Jaded appetites were always on the lookout for something new, but she would be very foolish indeed to imagine she could hold his interest for long. Still, to be aware of the danger of such a situation must remove most of its peril. There could be little harm in going with him, this once.

The night club was darkened. Guy ordered drinks and held her hand. The cabaret, the first performance of it, was halfway through. A woman sang, isolated in the ring of light on a small dais. The room was crowded and everyone's attention focused on the singer. Alana stared with the rest, noticing how the spotlight played on the girl's animated face and suggestively swaying body. All at once she felt depressed and thought regretfully of the less public career she had once set her heart on. Filled with unconscious apprehension, her eyes sought Guy's, only to find that he was already watching her.

'Scared?' he asked mockingly.

'Yes and no,' she answered evasively, knowing it would never do to tell him how much. 'After all, I should be used to it.'

As the last notes of music died away, the woman left the stage amidst a round of applause while a group of dancers took her place. Because she was more interested in the singer, Alana's brooding glance followed her and she was surprised when she paused beside their table.

'Hello, Guy,' she said huskily, placing a scarlet-tipped hand over his. 'Long time no see!'

'I've been busy,' he smiled, lifting her hand to his lips with a movement so smooth it shrieked to Alana of sheer expertise.

The girl patted his cheek, a gesture just as practised, but Alana noticed a tear in her eye as she moved on.

'Do you tell them all that?' she snapped.

'All what?' He regarded her hot face curiously.

'You've been too busy.'

'It's a painless excuse,' he raised a cynical eyebrow. 'Not with Mrs Brice, of course, she's different.'

'Did you know her well?' Alana's eyes were on the singer's retreating figure and she tried to suppress what she hoped wasn't a twinge of jealousy.

'Did you like her?' he countered.

Knowing he was referring to the girl's performance, she replied hesitantly, 'Half a song isn't much to go on, but she seems good. Very polished,' she added, with misgivings, thinking she wouldn't be nearly so accomplished.

'You all get that way in time,' he said dryly, reminding Alana that he considered her one of them. 'Come on,' he got to his feet, 'let's dance?'

The cabaret was over and couples were making for a small clearance on the floor. Guy wended his way between a few tables, pulling Alana by the hand he still held. Taking her in his arms as the band began a slow, dreamy number, he held her close, his chin resting on her mass of silk hair.

Despite herself awareness grew inside her and much as she tried to ignore it she was conscious of the faint masculine scent of him, the texture of his skin, the warmth and hardness of his body against hers.

'What are you afraid of?' he moved his chin an inch to ask softly. 'Haven't you been this close to a man before?'

She had been this close, but never so vulnerable, she thought in desperation. The chemistry between them was getting out of control. She had to escape.

But when she tried to pull away from him she found he was holding her too close to make escape possible. Then the hand on her shoulders began caressing her bare back, dropping lower to splay across the base of her spine, bringing her slender body intimately against his. Staring up at him, her blue eyes were feverish against the pallor of her skin, while her lower lip trembled.

She felt helpless as her eyelids fell and the touch of his mouth on her forehead brought a shaking weakness to her limbs. Perhaps there was no point in denying the attraction between them. There was just a chance that if she stopped fighting it, it might simply disappear. Guy Mason was a superb male specimen, and she wouldn't, she thought bitterly, be the first girl to fall for his sheer good looks. It was the hardness about him that frightened her, a hardness that had nothing to do with his undoubted physical strength.

Still holding her, he whirled her softly, exhibiting a not inconsiderable skill. He pulled her tighter and though she held herself as tautly as she could, she began to feel her body surrendering to the aching need he was arousing. When his right hand moved and began lightly caressing her hip, the breath left her throat in a strangled gasp.

'Stop it!' she pleaded.

'Stop what?' he murmured against her cheek, his hand stroking insidiously.

His warm breath made her quiver even more and gathering her wavering senses together she tried to push him away, but he only laughed mockingly and kissed her trembling mouth with a swift but calculated expertise.

'Don't worry,' he drawled, 'if I do decide to seduce you, Alana, I promise it won't be in quite such a public place.'

'You have an outsize opinion of yourself!' she retorted sharply, wishing her pulses would stop racing quite so madly. As the band finished playing he released her but kept his fingers on her wrist. From it he would be able to deduce how fast her heart was beating, but let him put it down to anger, she thought mutinously.

'Don't you think I could?' he mocked.

Surrounded by people, she dared defy him. 'Only if you used brute strength.'

'When the time comes I'll be surprised if I have to use any,' he drawled.

His confidence reduced her to silence, alarming her so much she didn't dare risk dancing with him again. When he asked, with a glint in his eye, and she refused, the glint deepened to open derision, but he didn't insist.

'I'd rather go home,' she said quickly, avoiding looking at him. 'I have to see Milo in the morning and I don't want to risk sleeping in.'

She thought he was about to tell her this was of no

consequence, but apparently he changed his mind. Allowing her her excuse, he didn't try to persuade her to stay any longer but took her straight back to Mrs Brice.

Alana didn't sleep well that night. Tossing and turning, she heard a clock in the distance chiming out the early hours of the morning; she thought it must be Big Ben. She began counting famous London landmarks instead of sheep, but still found it impossible to fall asleep. All of a sudden she hated London and wished she had never left Manchester.

Then reluctantly she admitted the real reason she couldn't sleep. Unhappily her thoughts turned to Guy Mason. He was older, not really her type, so why did she let him bother her, why was she attracted to him? She wasn't in love with him, but she couldn't honestly deny to herself that she might soon be, if she saw much more of him. And if she was foolish enough to fall for him there would be little chance of him ever returning her feelings. Although he had taken her out she was too young and unsophisticated to interest him seriously.

Since he had been responsible for getting her a job at the Remax she couldn't be rude to him, but she must try to avoid him. For her own peace of mind, more than anything else, but it would be better for both of them. He would be leaving the Remax when another hotel required his services and she didn't want to be left with a broken heart. Nor, she suspected, would he wish for any complications.

Yet, while she hoped he wouldn't be long in going, the thought of not seeing him again filled her with a curious despair. Ever since they had met she had felt drawn to him, and the attention he had continued to give her had done nothing to prevent this attraction from growing. He could make her tremble and he hadn't even kissed her. Just once, on the dance floor,

and then so briefly it shouldn't have meant anything—
so why did she yearn to be in his arms again?

Wearily Alana turned on her back and lay staring at
the ceiling, wondering why nothing seemed to make
sense. She didn't want to feel anything for Guy, but
when she thought of him travelling from one country
to another without a real home of his own, she was
conscious of a painful stab of pity. He must lead a
lonely life, despite having plenty of friends, but a man
who had come down in the world might have too much
pride to ask a woman to share it with him.

If they met again, for he had made no mention of
another meeting, she must make it clear that she
expected nothing from him. And at the same time make
sure he understood, once and for all, she wasn't in line
for a casual affair—if she hadn't already done so.

When she did fall asleep, she dreamt she was with
Guy. He was holding her tightly, moaning her name
while his kisses grew more and more passionate.
Fiercely she returned his kisses, winding her arms
around his neck, allowing him more licence than she
had ever permitted a man before. She woke with a
start, bathèd in sweat, to find it was well after nine,
and she had promised to be at the Remax by ten-
thirty.

If it was a major disaster that she was almost fifteen
minutes late, no one but herself appeared to think so.

'Hey, steady on!' Milo exclaimed, when she burst
into his office so hurriedly she nearly collided with a
chair. 'Nothing's worth breaking your neck over, darling. Not even me.'

'I'm sorry,' she gasped, regaining her breath, 'I
overslept.'

'Singers often do,' he said dryly, pouring her a mug
of coffee. 'Here, drink this and calm down—you're
better than most. Some just don't turn up for re-
hearsals at all.'

'And you forgive them?'

'Sometimes.'

Pushing back her thick hair impatiently, she exclaimed, 'I don't feel I qualify for such privileges yet, but I had such a time getting here. The tubes were full and I kept missing connections.'

'It will be better when you're living at the hotel,' he said.

Almost as if she had given him a cue, she thought wryly, and Guy was prompting him! Yet it had been a terrible hustle this morning, and if she didn't live at the hotel it was something she might have to face four times a day. 'I suppose you're right,' she admitted grudgingly.

Milo nodded. 'I'm busy seeing to it.'

Alana was startled that everything was being so swiftly taken out of her hands, but she had something more important on her mind. Glancing at him quickly, she asked anxiously, 'Did you—I mean, were they willing to let me have the money?' Catching a flicker of scepticism in his eyes, she flushed. 'I know I must sound awfully impatient, but once—once I have it I can send it off and forget about it.'

Reaching in one of his desk drawers, Milo took out a cheque and flipped it across to her. 'I hope so,' was all he said.

Her fingers trembling, Alana almost snatched it up, thrusting it in her handbag with a feverish murmur of thanks. She had an envelope already addressed to her parents, along with a note telling them she had managed to find a job and would be sending them something regularly. She couldn't ring them, for the telephone was something they had been forced to give up. She would post the letter, though, as soon as she could, and pray they received it quickly.

Milo still seemed to be considering her oddly. 'You

realise that management is putting a great deal of trust in you, giving you this?'

Alana frowned, having only thought of it as something to be paid back. What he said was true, of course. It was silly to feel it was an attack on her honesty.

'I'll repay every penny, I promise,' she assured him stiffly. 'I'll even give you a receipt.'

'No,' he refused quickly, 'no one's asked for that.' He hesitated. 'Haven't you ever thought, though, that this rather limits your freedom to leave us? If you should want to, that is.'

'It might also prevent you from sacking me,' she noted wryly.

'I don't think we'll be in a hurry to do that.'

She was grateful that Milo had obviously expressed sufficient confidence in her to the management to enable her to get an advance. She said so, and promised again, 'I won't let you down. I'll soon pay it off.'

When he nodded, she gave him such a dazzling smile his breath caught at the way it lit up her face. 'If you smile like that at the customers you'll have it paid off in no time,' he grinned, 'They'll be throwing silver and gold at your feet!'

'I'll share it with you,' she laughed, not for a moment taking him seriously as they moved into the empty nightclub and began working.

Milo kept her at it for the remainder of the morning. By one o'clock she decided ruefully that she had been stripped down to the basics. She felt like a small child starting school again, knowing nothing but that she had a lot to learn. Milo was no run-of-the-mill musician. He was brilliant, one of the best she was ever likely to meet. Whoever trained him had something to be proud of. If only he would let up a little, leave her some pride! It had probably taken him years to learn what he appeared to expect of her in five minutes.

'Okay, darling,' he relented eventually, 'you're better

than you think, so don't lose heart. I'm always striving for perfection and tend to forget I'm dealing with human beings.'

'You think we're blooming robots!' one of the band hooted derisively. 'You're a slave-driver!'

'I should think you're wasted here, Milo.' Alana managed a weak smile, her throat aching from sustained effort but managing to make herself heard above the forthcoming quips and laughter. The general atmosphere was good, she guessed none of them had anything to complain of, even if Milo worked them hard.

'I could be wasted if I were here all the time,' Milo replied, his warm brown eyes gleaming with amusement he did his best to hide.

Other members of the cabaret drifted in, and as he turned to talk to them Alana wondered what he meant. He introduced her briefly to the singer whom she would be replacing when the girl went abroad to join her husband at the end of the week.

After a few minutes she asked him—if he was finished with her, would it be all right to go to his office and collect her jacket? And would he mind if she went out to post a letter? He said it would be fine, but could she wait in his office until he had a word with her about this afternoon? He would be through here in a few minutes.

She left the door of the office open, but wasn't half way over the room before it closed behind her. Thinking Milo must have finished sooner than he had expected, she swung around, only to find herself staring straight at Guy Mason. He must have been right behind her and she hadn't seen him.

'Oh, hello,' she swallowed uncertainly. 'Aren't you busy?'

He paused, far too near for her liking, looking at her intently. 'I've been listening to you for the past hour.'

'I—see.' That would account for the mysterious prickles she had felt running down her spine, the same spine his fingers had lingered on so insistently the night before. Because she still felt disturbed by the memory, she said sharply, 'Hadn't you anything better to do?'

'Not this morning,' he smiled irritatingly. 'I've always had a weakness for sitting in dark woods listening to nightingales.'

'Lurking in a darkened night club listening to me could hardly be classed as the same thing.'

'I told Milo to lay off,' he muttered, his mocking grin fading as he studied her exhausted face.

'He only does his job,' she shrugged, 'and as it was my first morning perhaps I was over-anxious. You shouldn't encourage me to feel sorry for myself before I've even got started, Mr Mason. Anyway, I don't see why Milo should take any notice of you.'

Her tone was sharp, but when she imagined he was about to snap back, Guy's mouth merely twisted. 'Why indeed?' he murmured.

'I think,' she suggested carefully, 'it might be better if you stopped interesting yourself so much in what I'm doing. You could consider I'm no longer your responsibility. Everything seems to be going smoothly, and I'm sure I can manage anything else which might crop up.'

'Quite a speech!' he mocked, his eyes darkening with the anger she had sensed a moment ago.

With an uneasy sigh she turned to reach for her jacket, lying over a chair, but Guy caught hold of her. He swung her around, his hands on her arms, his glance stabbing the pure lines of her throat. For a few seconds he stood motionless, his icy grey eyes surveying her. Then, muttering something unflattering, he bent his head to brush his mouth over hers.

Alana knew she should pull away but was unable to

do so. Weakly she closed her eyes, trying not to tremble. She felt his lingering kiss on her mouth, then the tip of his tongue tracing the outline of it, while his right hand released its gentle grip on her chin to slip under her shirt and move swiftly across her breast.

He used no force, either with his mouth or hands, but she found his every movement unbearably exciting. Her mouth ached suddenly for the hardening pressure of his as her body became heated with an intense surge of desire.

That he withheld any signs of mounting passion suggested to Alana that he was merely teasing her. Yet by the time he raised his head to take possession of her slightly parted lips, she was tremblingly aware that he could have done anything he liked with her. If he had been able, there and then, to make love to her, she might not have uttered a word of protest.

A noise outside broke them apart, moments before Milo arrived. He didn't appear surprised to see Guy, as if he was used to having him around.

'Hello there,' he said.

Alana knew her cheeks were pink and was glad Milo wasn't looking at her closely. Before he did, to give herself an excuse for looking hot, she began struggling into her jacket. It wasn't such a good move, for Guy naturally came to her assistance, and the way his hands seemed to linger intimately made her face burn hotter than ever.

'Thank you,' she choked, jerking away from him.

Ignoring her silent protest, he stared coolly at Milo. 'I'm taking Alana out to lunch. Did you wish to speak to her about anything before we leave?' He took no more notice of Milo's quizzical glance than he did of Alana's indignant one.

He couldn't have listened to a word she had said! Before Milo could reply, she broke in, hoping he would read the appeal in her eyes correctly. 'I made no special

arrangements for lunch, Mr Sachs. If you want me
here . . .?'

'Oh, no no,' he exclaimed hastily, apparently blind
to her silent plea for help. 'It was only to give you the
times of a couple of appointments you have for this
afternoon. I made all the arrangements earlier.' From
his desk he picked up a card on which was written the
names of a famous beauty salon and a boutique.
Passing it to her, he grinned. 'See you aren't late, Miss
Hurst.'

As she reluctantly took the card, Alana wondered
why he had reverted to such deliberate formality. The
glint in Guy Mason's eyes surely couldn't have had
anything to do with it.

'Is this absolutely necessary?' she sighed. 'I usually
do my own hair, and I have dresses.'

'Absolutely necessary,' Milo replied.

With a shrug of resignation, she opened her handbag
and, on doing so, exposed the cheque lying where she
had left it. Closing it quickly, she hoped Guy hadn't
seen anything, although, as she assured herself, if he
had done he couldn't have known what it was about,
or had time to read the amount. She put the card in
her pocket instead, as he watched tight-lipped, but the
incident served to remind her that it was more imperative than ever to get rid of him, if she was to be
able to get the letter to her parents away before her
first appointment.

Guy had her through the door and out of a rear entrance almost before she realised she had moved. 'I
haven't time to have lunch with you,' she cried,
'Haven't I just told you, you don't have to keep on
looking after me as if I was a child! Besides,' she
panted, as he grasped her arm indifferently and
lengthened his stride 'I won't allow you to go on
spending money on expensive meals!'

'Something about you doesn't quite add up,' he

drawled laconically. 'Would you rather we stayed and had something at the hotel, on the house, if you like?'

'No! I mean, I haven't started yet. Not properly, anyway,' she protested. 'I wouldn't feel it was right, but you could.'

Again he glanced at her as though he couldn't make her out. 'Sorry,' he refused dryly.

'Well then,' she bit her lip in agitation, 'if you won't leave me on my own, I'll buy lunch . . .'

'As long as it's not fish and chips in the park!'

'It won't be.' She could think of few things she would like better, but didn't say so. Hastily, with another quick bite of her lip, which didn't go unnoticed, she decided she could just about manage with enough left over to see her through the rest of the week.

'It's uncommonly generous of you,' he smiled too ingratiatingly. 'Have you come into money?'

Angry colour rushed into her face at his sardonic tones. 'Yes,' she exclaimed recklessly, 'quite a lot. Although,' more cautiously, 'I don't want to spend it all on food. As I came in today I noticed a very reasonable place,' she glanced about her. 'I think it's just round the corner?'

She named a well-known chain of food bars and when Guy immediately agreed with her directions, she guessed he sometimes used them himself.

'Come on, then,' he sighed resignedly, 'anything to please the weaker sex.'

She was going to deny this hotly, then changed her mind. Why argue, when all she wanted was to have something quickly and in peace, so she could leave him!

'What would you like?' she asked, when they were seated in the popular establishment, with little room to spare at a narrow bench table. Guy's legs were so long he had to put them somewhere, but Alana wished she had somewhere else to put her own. Or that every time they touched each other she didn't have to catch her silly breath! 'Well, what have you decided on?' she insisted hollowly, as he studied the most expensive items on the menu.

'What have you?' he countered softly.

'Oh, just a sandwich and coffee.' She was ravenously hungry and fearing he might guess, felt compelled to express the most likely excuse. 'I can't afford to put on weight.'

'I see little reason for worry on that score,' he observed. 'But I'll have the same. I have a heavy afternoon ahead and perhaps I'll work better on an empty stomach.'

Need he be so sarcastic? Trying not to betray that she was aware of it, she went over to where piles of sandwiches were laid out under hinged Perspex covers. After removing some ham salad ones, she asked for two cups of coffee, all of which she paid for at the cash desk before returning to their table.

'It's very good of you,' Guy said solemnly, eyeing the solitary sandwich she set before him with a marked lack of interest.

Could there be anything worse, she thought irritably, than spending hard-earned money on someone who obviously didn't appreciate it? The sandwiches were a bit limp but not that bad. She tried to eat her own, but suddenly her appetite seemed to desert her and she wished she had given them both to him. Moodily she pushed her plate aside, concentrating on her coffee.

She was glad Guy didn't attempt to engage her in serious conversation but contented himself with a few remarks about the weather. He didn't actually say he enjoyed his lunch, but when he finished his own sandwich he reached over for hers, eating this as well.

Somehow it made her quiver inside. It reminded her of two lovers drinking from the same cup. As their eyes met she realised this might be his intention, for he held her gaze intently. It was as if he was forcefully reminding her of how she had felt when he had kissed her, and silently warning her not to try him too far. Not until she was actually shivering did he relent and look elsewhere.

As they were leaving the restaurant he said, 'I have a dinner engagement this evening, but before I go I'll ring to make sure you've managed to get home safely.'

Alana's blue eyes flashed impatiently. 'You aren't my keeper, Guy.'

Equally impatient, he snapped back, 'You shouldn't look as if you needed one, then. Have you any idea how to get to Lorraine's?'

How did he know where she was going? Milo hadn't mentioned any names, just handed her a card which she felt certain Guy hadn't seen. He hadn't been near enough to read what was on it, anyway. 'I was going to ask someone,' she admitted reluctantly.

'And how will you get there?'

Wishing he would stop asking such terse questions, she retorted sharply, 'I can walk. It can't be far.'

'You can't go as the crow flies in London,' he remarked dryly, hailing a taxi and thrusting her in it. While she protested wildly, he gave the driver instructions and a large enough note to cover the fare. 'See you, darling.' He looked straight in her face, daring her to deny him the same privileges she granted Milo.

While her hair was being restyled and shampooed she tried to bear it patiently. Her hair, thick and silky-soft, flowing past her shoulders when released from the tight little knot she usually wore it in, came in for a lot of admiration. The man who did it for her, Lorraine's top stylist, seemed unable to take his eyes off it.

'It's beautiful,' he said, 'like your face. You should appreciate your good fortune.'

'I'm a singer,' Alana returned wryly. 'People expect

me to look good, but I never spend much time on it.
I'd rather be doing something interesting, like swimming or walking in the rain.'

He looked so pained she felt almost ashamed of herself and to please him promised to wear her hair loose
from now on, instead of torturing it as he declared she
had been doing.

From the salon she went to the boutique. This she
found quite quickly as it wasn't far away. When she
emerged, an hour and a half later, she was the doubtful
owner of several smart evening gowns. One or two of
these were rather too smart for her liking, but apparently Milo had been on the phone with rough guide-
lines as to what she was to have. As in the beauty salon,
she felt she had no other choice but to submit. It wasn't
easy, she was discovering, to insist on her own way
when someone else was paying the bill.

CHAPTER FOUR

MRS BRICE was out when she returned and for once
Alana wasn't sorry. Going straight to her room, she sat
down on her unmade bed and to her horror burst into
tears. It must be due to the accumulated strain of
the past few days, but she couldn't seem to stop.
Eventually, feeling sure she could have no more tears
left, she dragged herself to the bathroom and washed
her swollen face.

Glancing in the mirror as she dried it, she realised
the havoc she had wrought. She had ruined all the
beautician's work. Oh, God, she thought, as a wave of
homesickness swept over her, what did it matter! She
wasn't cut out for this kind of life, why not admit it?
She liked singing but hated being stared at, and it

would be worse here, she suspected, then it had ever been in Manchester. If it hadn't been for her parents, that they needed the money, she would have chucked the whole thing. Could being unemployed really be worse than doing something one disliked?

When Mrs Brice came in from visiting a friend, she glanced keenly at Alana but forbore to say anything. If the girl's tenseness bothered her she kept it to herself. They had a cup of tea together, then Alana said she was going to bed. Not feeling like talking, she told Mrs Brice she was tired and could do with an early night. She didn't mention that Guy had promised to ring. As he hadn't, it was obvious he had forgotten.

Falling into an uneasy sleep after lying awake for some time, she woke with a start to feel a hand on her forehead, as if someone was testing her temperature, and opening startled eyes, she found herself gazing straight at Guy Mason.

As his face hovered above her, Alana sat up with a frightened cry, pushing his hand away. 'What on earth are you doing here?' she exclaimed. 'How—how dare you come into my bedroom?'

'Calm down. Blame your landlady,' he replied curtly. 'When I rang she told me she thought you were upset about something. She was worried, she thought you looked ill.'

'Why should she think that?' Alana muttered defiantly, very conscious that her ravaged face must supply the answer.

Deliberately he ignored the obvious. 'Did something go wrong this afternoon?' he asked bluntly.

'Not really,' she said tonelessly.

Sitting on the edge of the bed, since there wasn't a chair, Guy scrutinised her closed face narrowly. 'Come on, Alana, out with it. I'd have to be blind not to see you've been indulging in tears.'

Indulging! How like a man to use such a word! As if

tears were a luxury women should learn to do without.

'Most women weep at times,' she retorted, with a flippancy she could see annoyed him. 'I—I just felt like it,' she added, climbing down, as his mouth tightened ominously.

'I still want to know why,' he insisted softly.

Wearily she began brushing stray strands of hair from off her forehead, unaware of its beauty as the fair, silken tresses spread across her bare shoulders. Suddenly, as his glance made her conscious she was wearing only a thin nightdress, she flushed and grabbed a blanket.

Struggling underneath it, she again refused him a answer. 'You should have rung earlier, then you might have spared yourself the trouble of coming here.'

'It was no trouble,' he replied evenly. 'And I didn't ring earlier as the business I was dealing with this afternoon took so long I was already unforgivably late for my evening appointment.'

'You must have left her early, as well,' Alana couldn't resist observing, seeing it was only eleven.

His eyes flickered strangely at her faintly smug expression. 'It was a he, not a she.'

'Oh . . .' Alana stirred, moving her long, slender legs nervously. Guy looked so big and dangerously masculine she was afraid to let any part of her touch him.

'Scared?' he jeered softly, his eyes on her feminine form, clearly defined despite the blanket.

'No, I'm not?' she snapped coldly, striving to control her racing pulse. Here in the warm intimacy of the bedroom, she despised the thrill of tremulous excitement running through her at the sight of him sitting on her bed. Keeping her glance averted, she said, 'I appreciate your concern, and I'd be even more grateful if you'd take yourself out of here.'

'So you say.' He reached out lazily, his hands on her

shoulders, drawing her towards him.

Trying to hold the blanket in position, Alana lost her balance and fell right into his arms. Speaking against the top of her head, he drawled mockingly, 'You won't tell me what's wrong—and perhaps it's nothing much, but I believe you need comforting.'

She tried to escape, but he was too strong for her, and when her strength gave out she resorted to pleading, 'Please, Guy, why won't you just go?'

'I will in a few minutes, when you're feeling better.'

'How can I feel better,' she whispered incoherently against his broad chest, 'while you're with me?'

'Shall I show you?' he murmured derisively. Turning her face up to meet his lips, he kissed her sore eyes one after the other. His mouth was cool and firm, oddly soothing. At least it was until he reached her lips. As she responded, for all her resolve not to, by winding her arms around his neck, he captured her mouth in a kiss which threatened to ravage her very soul.

Then he was lying on the bed beside her without her having any idea how he had got there, and somehow his kisses were driving all knowledge of his exact movements from her head. The blanket fell, his hands pushing aside the thin straps of her nightdress until it joined the blanket round her waist. Following it, his hands slid to cup the silky softness of her small breasts and he raised his mouth from hers to gaze down on them.

'God, you're so beautiful,' he breathed huskily, 'You look cool and untouched, so virginal. I want you—I can't sleep for thinking of you. Nights are a torment ——' As his voice trailed off thickly, his mouth moved along her throat, over the soft white skin to taste the rosy peaks which tipped the pale mounds so expressively.

'You want me, too?' he muttered, humiliatingly able,

from expert experience, to judge her reactions exactly.

Alana felt a feverish flush staining her cheeks and was incapable of handling her own emotions. She could only lie mutely in his arms, her mouth soft and shaking, wholly at the mercy of feelings completely new to her. So new that she hadn't the faintest notion how to cope with them, as her physical desires fought for total mastery over her mental ones.

As Guy held her, she convulsively tightened her own arms about him, her fingers digging into his thick, dark hair to press him even closer as his mouth devoured her. Passionately she twisted, not bothering to deny what he said, trying to get as near to him as possible.

Lifting his head, he touched her face with unsteady hands as she lay half under him. Then his caresses became softer, more sensuous, and she could feel the jerky movements of his body as he pulled off his jacket.

Alana . . .,' he groaned savagely.

She was clinging to him blindly when the door opened. 'Mr Guy!' Mrs Brice exclaimed, her voice so full of sharp disapproval, it succeeded in piercing the flood of feeling which was making them both unaware of anything else.

With a deep sigh, Guy rested his head on Alana's shoulder. 'All right, Joan, I get the message. I'll be with you in a moment. Just get out of here, will you?'

As the door closed again with a resounding bang, he grimaced wryly and eased himself carefully off the bed. 'I'm sorry,' he muttered, 'I should have remembered we weren't alone.'

Wildly Alana recovered her blankets, although such a move did little to hide her embarrassment. To her dismay she found she was trembling. 'Why didn't you explain to her?' she whispered frantically.

'Explain what?' he asked dryly. 'How my good intentions went astray? How I almost came to take advantage of her little ewe lamb? And, in turn, you might have had to find some excuse for your obvious willingness to stay in my arms.'

'Oh, just leave me alone! I think I hate you!' she cried, angry frustration saving her mercifully from the tears which threatened to fall again. She didn't want to even think about her own response, let alone discuss it. It was better not to.

That his face softened suddenly almost proved her undoing. Swiftly he bent to tilt her averted chin, to drop a deep but tender kiss on her unsteady mouth. 'That's just to prove how much I hate you,' he mocked softly. 'Goodnight, my sweet. I'll see you tomorrow.'

During the next two weeks Alana saw him every day. Usually Milo spent a few hours with her each afternoon. Sometimes the band was there, sometimes not, and when it wasn't he usually accompanied her on the piano or whatever musical instrument was best suited to the kind of song she was singing. He seemed able to play just about anything, and she often marvelled at the diversity of his talents. He interested her as a person although he didn't attract her as a man.

She would liked to have known more about him, but he told her little, only that he liked to travel occasionally. When she asked Guy about him he was equally vague. 'He's a good chap and I like him, but I know very little about his personal life. Why so curious?'

Could Guy be jealous? She felt an odd twinge of shame for hoping he was, but dismissed it as improbable. Sometimes she found herself wishing they hadn't met on the train, for it was difficult to tell if his protective attitude was solely because of what had happened then or because he genuinely liked her. Each day he came to hear her sing, she knew at once when he arrived, even when she didn't see or hear him. It was a kind of mental telepathy combined with a definite prickle down her spine. Secretly she called it her built-in alarm system, but trying to joke about it she failed. To be so aware of a man might mean she was getting too fond of him, and this was the last thing she wanted to happen. Her life was complicated enough as it was!

He took her out to dinner twice but didn't attempt to kiss her again, which made Alana wonder anxiously if he regretted having done so before. The question of dancing with him didn't arise either, as the restaurants he took her to didn't run to a band or appear to bother with any other kind of music. They were quiet, out-of-the-way places, and so modest that she stopped nagging him about being extravagant. After all, he probably earned a fairly decent salary and could afford to go somewhere occasionally.

On the Saturday she moved to her new room in the hotel she thought he might have offered to help, but he didn't. Not that she could complain about any lack of assistance. A taxi had been sent to collect her and she hadn't been allowed to touch one piece of luggage. Everything had been carried to her room for her; there had even been a maid to do her unpacking, something Alana would rather have done herself.

'I have my instructions, miss,' the girl said, and Alana hadn't liked to argue. She couldn't help wondering, though, who had given the instructions, because she found it difficult to believe hotels usually cosseted their singers to this extent. Maybe Milo had asked them to do it, for, like Guy, he seemed to have formed the impression that she needed looking after.

It wasn't until after she had showered and was wandering around her small sitting-room trying to decide what to wear that Guy appeared. Milo had advised her to come and watch the show that evening as she was to be on herself on Monday. She had brushed her hair until it shone, but hadn't yet done her face as it was still early. Having broken a nail, she

was busy filing it and thinking about her dress when
Guy's knock came.

He was leaning against the doorpost, and when she
answered the door he smiled and asked, 'Aren't you
going to invite me in?'

Uncertainly Alana smiled back. She had known he
had a room in the hotel and wondered where it was.
Somehow the thought of his room being near hers
filled her with a delicious kind of apprehension.

'Well, aren't you?' teasingly his glance rested on her
bemused face.

'Oh yes, of course!' she exclaimed. 'That is,' she
hesitated, stammering, 'I'm not sure that I should.'

'Ask me in, you mean? Is that what you're trying to
say?' When she nodded unhappily, his grin widened.
'You fear they might throw you out, if you're found
entertaining a man in your room?'

'Well, mightn't they?' She felt hurt because of his
mocking tones and stung to retort, 'It's a very nice set
of rooms. When I had to leave Mrs Brice I never
dreamed I'd be given anything so nice. I've my own
bedroom, bathroom and lounge. It's small, but even
you must agree it sounds almost too good to be true.'

'Oh, I don't think you'll be asked to give it up in a
hurry,' he said smoothly, placing his hands on her
waist and lifting her bodily aside, so he could enter the
room and close the door. He silenced her strangled
gasp by adding, 'The manager himself asked me to
make sure you have everything you require. It's all
part of my job.'

'Oh, I see,' she faltered, feeling she might have made
a fool of herself. 'Well, that does make a difference, I
suppose. I had no idea.'

'I'll forgive you,' he chuckled. 'And are you satisfied?'

'I'd be a fool if I wasn't,' she replied dryly, 'If
only . . .'

'Yes, if only what?' he asked softly as she paused.

'I know it sounds silly,' she whispered, tightening the sash of her robe nervously, 'but the thought of singing to a packed London night club makes me want to run away. It's so different from Manchester.'

'When do you go on?' he asked tersely, noting the dark smudges beneath her wide blue eyes.

'Day after tomorrow.' She tried to take hold of herself and speak lightly. 'I expect it's only nerves.'

'Maybe you won't have to do it for ever,' he said slowly, staring at her.

'I hope not,' she sighed.

'Look,' his voice suddenly hardened, 'it's what you chose, isn't it? There are other things but only you can make the decision. Say the word and I'll tell Milo to find a replacement.'

'No!' A sharp panic assailed her as she remembered her parents. Oh, God . . .!

'Then save me the histrionics,' he snarled, as if he would liked to have slapped her.

Turning from him, Alana went white. She realised she was at fault, but his harsh anger was like a blow. 'I'm sorry,' she whispered.

'So you should . . . Oh, hell, what's the use!' he groaned as she shivered. 'Listen, Alana,' he checked the time on his watch, 'I think what you're really suffering from is nerves, and a change of scene might help. I have a cottage in the country, where I'm going for the weekend. Why not come with me, you can pack anything necessary in a few minutes. I'll guarantee,' he assured her softly, 'you won't regret it.'

As he finished speaking, Alana stared at him, not knowing how to answer. He was attractive enough to cause any girl to lose her head. Tonight he was wearing his favourite jeans with a casual shirt. Her heart missed a beat and began racing. If she spent the weekend with him how would he ensure she wouldn't regret it? A flame ran amok in her body and her knees almost buckled.

'Do your parents live there?' she asked slowly.

'They're both dead,' he replied.

'We'd be alone?'

'Yes.' He paused, his mouth tightening, reading all the doubts on her uncertain face. 'I asked you there to relax, Alana, nothing else.'

She gripped the sash of her robe tightly to prevent her hands trembling, realising she couldn't accept. Guy might be asking her to trust him, but could she trust herself? His attraction, his whole personality, threatened to sweep her off her feet. How much harder would it be to resist him if they were alone together and the pulsating awareness between them somehow got out of hand?

She drew a breath with difficulty, her throat closing up. 'I—it's good of you to suggest it, but I promised Milo I would see the show tonight, and I can't let him down.'

Guy stared at her unmoving. 'I can easily make it all right with him.'

'But what would you say?' she faltered, her cheeks colouring. 'He'd guess.'

His lips curled. 'Come on, Alana, don't tell me you're afraid of a little gossip! But there wouldn't be any, I can assure you.'

'I—I still can't,' she insisted.

His eyes travelled over the tense features of her face. 'A pity.'

'I'm sorry.'

'If you were half as sorry as I am you would agree to go.'

Irony tinged his voice and she didn't like it. He was a masterful twister of words, making her feel she was letting him down. Her eyes clung to his. In them she read many things, but no great despair. A sudden sick suspicion struck her. 'Will you take someone else?'

'No.'

Joy pulsed through her veins, yet the thought of Guy alone in his humble cottage made her heart ache as it had done when she had contemplated his loneliness on a previous occasion. Her compassion urged her to throw her arms about his neck and give in. It was the strictness of her upbringing that provided the restraint to hold back.

The smile didn't quite reach his eyes. 'My answer obviously pleases you—are you sure you won't change your mind?'

When she shook her head, he sighed. 'So much determination in such a little bundle! Well, if you won't, I'd better say goodbye, otherwise I won't reach my cottage until midnight and the lane leading to it isn't the best to negotiate in the dark.'

Having expected him to leave immediately, she was startled when his arms reached out to pull her close. And she let him, even when the glittering devil in his eyes warned her she might regret it.

'Kiss me,' he muttered. 'Aren't I entitled to at least some compensation?'

How could she refuse? A conciliatory warmth kept her still as his arms encircled her, but couldn't disguise the racing of her pulses, nor her yielding response. Guy silently commanded her obedience and without a struggle she gave in, closing her eyes as she followed the dictates of his will.

His kisses sent spasms of delight through her body and she felt desire rising in her, sharp and swift. Her muscles clenched in their sheath of protective innocence, then melted as his hand pulled her head back and he buried his mouth in her throat. She trembled as he nibbled a direct path up her neck to her ear. He traversed all the most sensitive areas. There were some places she could scarcely bear him touch, so fiercely did they increase her already heightened sense of arousal. Yet all the while she waited with quickening breathing, her lips hungering for the touch of his.

The first contact was so gentle she scarcely felt it, yet for a few seconds it was enough. His mouth closing over hers was oddly beautiful. She had a breathless feeling of being borne up on wings, of soaring above all earthly things. Because Guy didn't apply any immediate pressure she grew more confident, parting her lips to allow the intimate exploration of his, and her hands to seek the warmth of his flesh.

As her fingers crept tentatively under his shirt, his mouth altered. It hardened, swiftly taking over control, ruthlessly parting her lips, then softening to begin a deeper probe. Again a sense of timelessness enveloped her, taking away all sense and reason.

Alana surrendered with an eager willingness, suddenly possessed of a craving so strong it was rendering her mindless, and he played on her emotions like a master fiddler. Each rational thought, as it reared its head, was overwhelmed by passionate desire, and he must have guessed she was ready to give him anything he wanted from the way she clung to him.

She heard his breath quicken as he parted her robe, lightly stroking her hips and the tops of her legs. Then sharply asserting a control he seemed in danger of losing, his hands swung quickly across her back to caress her shoulders.

Feelings inside Alana began changing alarmingly. Her eyes grew heavy as a burning sensation crept along her veins, licking tiny flames into a raging inferno in the pit of her stomach. She wasn't sure where her own hands were, but her fingers dug into his mucles, as he felt her response, and again began shaping her slender limbs to the hardening contours of his. He proceeded with a savage disregard for any hurt he might be inflicting.

She gave a smothered gasp as his restraint disappeared and her body blended with his. Like a puppet she obeyed him, striving blindly to satisfy the increasing demands he made. His mouth plundered until the skin of her lips fractured beneath the impact of his teeth. Then, as if to make completely sure of her, his right hand closed tightly over her left breast.

It was an unequal contest. Alana knew when the battle was lost and saw no sense in making a secret of her defeat. If Guy hadn't already guessed, he soon would, how essential he was becoming to her very existence. Ways of showing him how much she cared were suggested to her, but it was her body speaking, not her mind. Her mind was working only enough to register the total depth of her commitment.

When she thought he was about to lift her and take her to bed, it was nothing short of sheer deprivation to find herself put firmly and suddenly away from him. As his arms released her she might have fallen if he hadn't thrust her gently into the nearest chair.

'You don't want an affair any more than I do.' he said tersely, as she raised bewildered eyes. 'You couldn't cope with the situation.'

A little sense returned as Alana collapsed against the soft cushions, but not enough to prevent a small cry of protest escaping her. 'Please, Guy . . .?' she whispered.

He straightened abruptly, avoiding her dazed, pleading glance. As he moved away from her, his pale face bore the unmistakable lines of a rigidly imposed discipline. Then, as his control strengthened, it was replaced by his usual sardonic expression. When he turned he looked no more moved than he might have done if they had been sitting discussing the weather.

'Don't say anything more, little one,' he advised softly. 'Just be good while I'm away and I'll see you on Monday.'

As Alana dressed her thoughts were bitter. What a

fool she was! Guy had kissed her and she had completely lost her head, while he had been able to call a halt just when it suited him. His reference to an affair had been brief but brutal. There was a lot he hadn't said, obviously expecting her to read between the lines. He wasn't averse to a few kisses, but anything of a more lasting nature, which might lead to complications, was out. He travels fastest who travels alone, would be Guy Mason's motto!

She wore one of her own dresses and used very little makeup, hoping to go unnoticed when she went down to the night club. After dinner, which she was scarcely able to touch, she decided she might as well go and get it over with.

Milo escorted her to a secluded table, but was able to stay with her only a few minutes before having to leave. Without him, she felt slightly conspicuous on her own, but gave a start of alarm when someone slipped into the chair Milo had just vacated.

'I'm sorry, that's reserved,' Alana said stiffly, not wishing the man, who was regarding her with interest, to imagine she was an easy pick-up.

'Oh, Milo won't mind,' he smiled, making her realise he must have watched her come in. 'He knows me.'

'But I don't,' she replied sharply. She had never seen him before, she was sure. He might not have stood out in a crowd, the way Guy did, but he was tall and very elegant to look at.

'You must allow me to correct that,' to her surprise he introduced himself immediately, 'I'm Fabian Marlow,' he held out a slender, gold-ringed hand, 'and you're Alana Hurst, Milo's new singer.'

'How did you know that?' she gasped, while her fingers were crushed in an astonishingly firm grasp.

'Don't be alarmed,' he grinned shamelessly. 'I asked.'

'Who?'

'The girl who's singing now, the one you're going to replace. I was with her when you arrived, a few moments ago.'

'So if your curiosity is satisfied,' she told him dryly. 'feel free to leave.'

'Oh no, it isn't,' he said hastily, like a small boy refusing to be thwarted. 'I want to know a lot more. For instance, how did Milo discover you?'

'He didn't——' She hesitated. If he was a friend of Milo's he probably knew Guy. 'Mr Mason gave me an introduction.' Which was all she was going to say!

'Mr—Mason?' Fabian's brown brows creased. 'You don't mean Guy?'

'Yes.' She glanced at him warily, puzzled by the faint amusement in his face. 'What's so funny?' she asked with unusual tartness.

'Nothing. I'm sorry,' he smiled soothingly, 'it was just that I'm not used to hearing him called Mr Mason.'

'I'm afraid I don't follow,' but she felt something inside her tauten, as if getting ready to receive a blow.

'You probably don't.' For the first time Fabian looked a trifle uncertain. 'Mason is Guy's second Christian name, which I believe he occasionally uses as a surname when he doesn't want it to be known who he really is.'

Alana's lips grew so stiff she found it difficult to move them. Shock ricocheted through her, whitening her face to a frozen mask. 'Who is he really?' she asked, fearing she knew the answer even before she asked.

Fabian Marlow viewed her a trifle anxiously. 'You really want to know?'

As she nodded dully, he said, 'He's Guy Mason Renwick.'

'And he owns this hotel?'

'Yes, and a lot of others like it, in different parts of the globe.'

Alana stared at him, failing to hide, that she was completely stunned by what she had just heard. How could Guy have deceived her like this? What a fool she had been! Hollowly she wondered how many times she had called herself one since they'd met, yet only now did she feel she really deserved the title. Why hadn't she had the sense to realise who he was? Mere employees didn't achieve what he had achieved. A man who worked casually for a hotel would never have the authority to do what he had done. Getting her a job, a room, instant acceptance. She had thought he must have a magic wand, while she should have guessed . . .!

When Fabian put a sympathetic hand over hers she scarcely realised what he was doing. 'Alana?' he said sharply, anxiously.

'I'm sorry,' she tried to smile but couldn't, 'I've been so stupid, you see. I thought Guy—Mr Renwick, that is—just worked here.'

He squeezed her hand gently. 'Don't worry, I understand. I always get a shock when something like this happens to me. I remember when I first started off in my first job. I was telling a young man, whom I liked the looks of, exactly what I thought of the old fogey in the other office, meaning my boss. Unfortunately the lad turned out to be his son. Of course I got the sack, but that decided me to start out on my own. Point of story,' he grinned, 'things are never as black as they seem. Look at me, a self-made millionaire, while I might still have been sitting in that corny office.'

A lot of what he was saying had escaped her, as angry thoughts refused to allow much else to sink in. This time she did manage to raise a small smile, which appeared to satisfy him.

'Where is Guy tonight, by the way?' Fabian, as though giving her a moment to compose herself, glanced around. 'I know it isn't one of his usual haunts, but I have seen him here before.'

'He's gone to his country cottage for the weekend,' Alana replied, finding it difficult to believe that only an hour ago Guy had held her in his arms and asked her to go with him to his—humble abode!

'Ah, his country cottage,' Fabian smiled, 'and his merry widow, I presume?'

'Merry—what?' she whispered, thinking she might as well hear it all. Nothing could surely make the hurt worse than it was?

'His next-door neighbour,' Fabian was not apparently reluctant to explain. 'She's been there since he bought the place, first as the neighbour's wife, then his widow, but always with her eye on Guy. So far he's withstood her advances, but one of these days I'm sure he'll give in, once he realises he's pushing thirty-seven—or is it eight? Veronica Templeton's about the same age, you see, so if they want a family they might have to hurry.'

When she had asked Guy, he'd said he wouldn't be taking anyone else. He hadn't bothered to explaind that he had someone there already! Someone so easily available that Alana's refusal hadn't disturbed him unduly. She felt so furious she could have killed him, if he'd been sitting opposite her instead of Fabian.

She found it difficult to get through the rest of the evening as the depression that settled on her refused to go away. Another time it might have disturbed her that Fabian Marlow seemed unable to take his eyes off her, but Guy's betrayal, as she chose to call it, left her strangely unaware of what other people were saying and doing. She would liked to have gone straight to her suite, but dared not risk it. Once there her anger might only become worse, and already it was threatening to tear her in two.

When eventually she rose to leave, Fabian, to her dismay, asked if he could take her out the next day.

'If you haven't any other engagements,' he smiled, 'we can go wherever you like.'

She thanked him, but asked if he would give her a ring in the morning, by which time she hoped he might have changed his mind. She didn't want to get involved with another man.

Unfortunately he appeared to think her request quite reasonable and jotted down her telephone number, which she saw no sense in withholding as he had apparently discovered, along with everything else he had taken pains to find out about her, that she lived at the hotel.

When he did ring it was barely eight and she was shaken out of her sleep in surprise. 'What an hour!' she complained.

'I didn't make a fortune lying in bed,' he replied.

How he enjoyed reminding her of it! 'I'm still undecided,' she said.

'Oh, come on!' he laughed.

'I suppose I could.' Wouldn't anything be better than spending the day alone, letting the insidious thoughts, which had tortured her almost non-stop throughout the night, carry on with their work? Fabian was young and cheerful and talked a lot, she wouldn't have time to think.

They spent the whole day together and Alana knew, if she hadn't been so agitated over Guy, she would have enjoyed it. They explored London as she felt she couldn't bear to go into the country. Fabian was very attentive and she found herself beginning to like him. On the telephone, she had asked him bluntly if he was married and he had said he wasn't, but she didn't ask any more personal questions. If she had it might only have led him to believe she was growing interested in him, which she wasn't. To be deceived once was enough. If she allowed it to happen again she would only have herself to blame!

CHAPTER FIVE

ALANA was so tired that night she slept heavily and woke late with a headache. When she saw Milo after lunch he was unimpressed with her pale, shadowed face.

'You aren't worrying about tonight, are you?' he exclaimed. 'I can assure you there's no need.'

'No, of course not,' she replied, perhaps a shade too hurriedly. 'I had a headache, but it's gone.'

'I hope so,' he said, frowning.

'Have you seen—er—Guy?' Hoping he hadn't noticed her hesitation, she pretended to be searching for something in her bag.

There was a pause while Milo obviously tried to decide if that was what was bothering her. 'You know he's out of town?'

'Yes. At his cottage.'

'He's probably been delayed,' said Milo. 'It certainly looks like it, because I haven't seen him around this morning.'

'When do you think he'll be back?' she asked, striving to make it sound like an idle query.

'Oh,' Milo shrugged carelessly, 'you never can tell, maybe today or tomorrow?'

Alana thought she might have done better if she could have delayed her first performance until after she had seen Guy. She had such a load of resentment on her mind she found it difficult to concentrate on anything else. Whichever way she looked at the situation she came to the same conclusion, and it hurt. Guy had tricked her, not only about himself but into falling in love with him. It seemed to Alana that he had given her a job in his hotel and made a deliberate assault on her senses without giving her a chance to look for anything elsewhere. If she hadn't been so gullible she might have guessed that he amused himself with girls like herself, while his real affection and respect was given to one special woman.

Milo had told her briefly the kind of thing he would like her to wear that evening, but left the final choice to Alana. When she chose one of her more demure dresses he didn't object, in fact he seemed very pleased with the results.

'You'll do!' he smiled, his eyes appraising her slim, supple figure, her delicate face and long, slender neck which balanced the weight of her shining hair to perfection. 'You look young and beautiful, darling. Just go out there and smile at them and you'll bowl them over.'

'Will I really do?' she asked anxiously. 'I have to be more than a pretty face, you know.'

'You will be,' he promised happily.

Amazingly, or so it seemed to Alana, she was a success. It stunned her how, after her first number, her audience clamoured for more. She had no illusions about her voice, it was pleasant and nicely pitched, but nothing outstanding. It must be the sexy tone which Milo spoke of but she couldn't hear, she thought wryly, but it wasn't until after her second song, when again she was given a huge round of applause, that she really began to feel confident. Then Milo said she would be on again later and she retired to her dressing-room.

When she returned Fabian Marlow was one of the first to congratulate her. His blue eyes, so warm and friendly, acted like a balm on the soreness of her heart, and he stayed with her for the remainder of the evening. She found his gentle, undemanding companionship more than acceptable after Guy's deception.

She didn't see Guy until late the next night, after she had finished singing and gone upstairs to her suite. She had known he was back when she felt the familiar prickle which always told her of his presence. He had been sitting at a table, alone, but she had only glanced at him once. Afterwards she had kept her eyes averted and tried to control her racing pulse.

He didn't pursue her to the dressing-room, but he did follow her upstairs. Guessing he might, she waited, opening the door when he knocked.

His rap on the door had been impatient, but his eyes were smiling when he looked down on her. 'Hello,' he said softly. 'Missed me?'

If her life had depended on it, Alana couldn't have spoken. Her heart seemed somewhere in her mouth and her tongue incapable of moving. Numbly she stood aside, turning to follow him as he walked past her. When she didn't speak he must have thought it was because she was so pleased to see him, for he still looked happy as he turned again to face her.

'If you're very nice to me,' he teased, 'I might just forgive you for ignoring me down there. Why didn't you come and sit beside me after you finished singing, instead of rushing up here?'

Taking a deep breath, Alana clasped her hands tightly behind her back to prevent them trembling. 'I—I'm sorry, Mr Renwick,' she managed to emphasise his name coldly. 'I had no idea you wanted me to.'

He stiffened. If Alana hadn't been so angry, she might have laughed at the flicker of dismay which crossed his face. Then his surprise disappeared, to leave only an expressionless mask. 'Who told you?'

'At least you don't deny it,' she countered bitterly.

'What would be the use?' he said tersely. 'But you haven't answered my question. Who told you? I want to know!'

'Someone at the hotel. Not Milo,' she hastened to add.

Making no attempt to defend himself, Guy looked at her closely. 'It doesn't really matter, I suppose. You had to find out some time.'

'You could have told me yourself, though,' she retorted furiously, 'instead of letting me make a fool of myself!'

'Why should you feel I was trying to make a fool of you?' he frowned.

'Well, weren't you?' she snapped, glaring at him.

'No,' he replied coolly, his eyes narrowing at her tone but still controlling his temper. 'Why should I?'

'For amusement, most probably,' she flung back, thinking for sheer audacity he could never be matched, 'You deceived me from the start . . .!'

'Now wait a minute,' he cut in, his sardonic tones crisping before the rage in her face. 'Wasn't it you who approached me on the train, crying for help, which I believe I gave. How do you label that deception?'

'I wasn't referring to that!' she cried, getting more worked up by the minute. 'It began when you pretended to be someone other than you are, and gave the impression you were as poor as myself. You said you knew where I might find a room. I suppose you own the house Mrs Brice lives in, as well as everything else?'

When he nodded grimly, she scarcely paused for breath before rushing on. 'That's when you must have started laughing at me!' When he neither confirmed or denied this but appeared to be waiting to hear what she had to say next, she didn't hesitate. 'You had a friend, you said, who worked in a hotel, who might give me a job? Your employee, Mr Renwick, your hotel! How do you explain the deviousness of that?'

'Would you have had anything to do with the job if I'd told you the truth?' he asked flatly, his eyes on her hot cheeks. 'You were so bristling with prickly pride and independence, you would never have come within miles of the hotel if you'd known I was the owner.'

'You could have given me the chance,' she said sharply. 'If you'd bothered to explain properly I might have understood.'

'Would you?' he asked dryly.

Much as she hated the doubt in his voice, Alana hated even more to think he could be right. Her temper, however, enabled her to ignore everything but her own painful sense of injustice.

'Milo must have been laughing his head off, along with heaven knows how many others!'

Coldly, Guy replied, 'Milo knew nothing except that I didn't want you to know who I was.'

'But why?' she cried wildly.

Cynically he shrugged. 'Maybe I wanted to be loved for myself for a change.'

Pain stabbed right through her, removing any lingering discretion. 'I'd rather you left love out of it,' she retorted through set lips, 'especially since you've been spending the weekend with another woman!'

All signs of tolerance died instantly from his face, to be replaced by a anger as great as her own. 'Someone has been busy!' he sneered. 'What else did your kindly informant tell you?'

Just that you're going to marry her, Alana almost said, but didn't. Her teeth snapped shut in time. It wouldn't be fair to betray Fabian's confidences so far. She hadn't been able yet to establish exactly how friendly Fabian and Guy were, but if they shared a close friendship she felt she had no right to do anything which might destroy it.

'Can you deny you've spent the weekend with another woman?' she challenged instead.

'Why should I?' His mouth curled. 'It would only be wasting valuable time when I'm sure you can't wait to air your other grievances.'

It hurt so much that he didn't deny he had been with Veronica Templeton that Alana's fury increased irrationally. 'You seem to think I have nothing to complain about!' she snapped.

'No, I don't think you have,' his eyes were frosty with contemptuous anger. 'Instead of feeling so sorry for yourself, why not begin counting your blessings? If I withheld part of my name and it annoys you, I apologise. But you certainly exaggerate the rest.'

Refusing to let him get away with this, she exclaimed, 'You told me yourself you worked here!'

'Yes, damn it, woman,' he made an obvious effort to speak lightly, 'I do. When I'm here I probably work harder than anybody.'

'All right, I'll word it differently,' she cried, incensed that he twisted everything she said. 'You implied that you were one of your own employees, and you couldn't afford lunch.'

'It was you who implied that,' he reminded her acidly.

She refused to listen. 'I suppose it was you who arranged for me to have this suite?'

'And if I did?' he asked grimly.

'Then everyone would be aware you'd provided it, except me!' she flashed him a venomous glance. 'What can they be thinking?'

'That I visit you each night,' he taunted, 'as my quarters are just along the corridor.'

As her eyes widened with horrified comprehension, he gave a sudden groan and pulled her to him, the anger dying from his face. 'What a storm in a teacup!' he teased, gently brushing her hair back from her hot cheeks. 'You were so lovely tonight, my sweet, I couldn't wait to tell you, yet here we are quarrelling about something so trivial as to be scarcely worth mentioning in the first place.'

Frantically she pushed away from him, terrified of

her traitorous longing to stay in his arms and angry that he dismissed his amazing duplicity as trivial. As she struggled to be free of him, her hand caught his face, her nail tearing a jagged cut in the hard skin. The blood ran and fright swept over her as she glimpsed his livid expression.

'You little vixen!' he snarled, releasing her.

Almost choking, she retorted, 'I hate you—you can keep your room and your job! I'm leaving first thing in the morning!'

He looked blazingly angry, and there could be no doubt at all that he was taking her very seriously now. 'I think not, Miss Hurst,' the leaping fury in his eyes contrasted strangely with the ice in his voice. 'Tomorrow you will certainly be out of here, as fast as I can arrange it, but only to another room.'

'I want to leave!' she whispered hoarsely.

Adamantly he shook his head, staring at her with such extreme distaste she found it difficult to connect him with the man she had previously known.

'Why do you think,' he went on ruthlessly, 'I didn't tell you who I really was at the beginning, or at least after Milo said you could actually sing and he'd be happy to employ you? Because he also told me you'd asked for a loan of five hundred pounds—to cover debts you owed.'

'He—told you?' Alana couldn't remember ever going so cold with shock. She had forgotten all about the money.

'How else do you imagine you got the cheque? I was the only one willing to give you that kind of money.'

'It—it came from the hotel.'

'Naturally,' he snapped, 'but I had to authorise it.'

Unable to think straight, she made another mistake. 'You gave it to get me in your power.'

'My God!' he exclaimed furiously, 'you're going to regret accusing me of that! I let you have it so you could pay off your debts, nothing more or less. It's a long time since, if ever I can recall such an occasion, anyone made a fool of me, and you can congratulate yourself you succeeded. I imagined, as you'd been unemployed, you'd inadvertently got into some kind of financial trouble. I may have enough myself, but I'd be damned insensitive if I didn't realise thousands haven't. Giving you money, though, rather tied my hands, did it not, regarding telling you who I really was? If you'd known, you would never have accepted a penny.'

'Of course not!' she mumbled, on a horrified gasp.

'So,' he snarled, without one iota of pity for her sheet white face and tortured eyes, 'you hate me maybe as much as I despise myself for trying to save your mercenary little neck. But as for leaving, my girl, much as I'd like to see the back of you, you'll stay until you've cleared off every cent! And, with interest, it's going to take some time! I'll see you in the morning.'

The way he slammed the door almost lifted it from its hinges. The noise seemed to shudder through the hotel and Alana, and she sank in a miserable little heap on the carpet. Burying her face in her arms against the deep cushions of an armchair, she felt too miserable for tears. Why hadn't she remembered about the money? After discovering Guy's real identity she should have guessed it had come from him. It seemed inconceivable that she had forgotten all about it, and she couldn't really blame him for believing she had intended walking out without making any arrangements to repay it.

She sighed, a deeply tremulous sound. A moment before he'd slammed out, she had heard him mutter something about deriving no joy from deceiving her. And since he had explained about the money, she could understand he had been in something of a dilemma. What she couldn't understand was why he had continued being kind to her and taking her out. Of course she didn't have to use a lot of intelligence to come up with a probable answer, but she could be wrong. Then as she recalled he was going to marry another woman, she realised she couldn't be. A man like Guy Renwick would only amuse himself with a night club singer.

Still, a voice whispered in her heart, it had been inexcusable to condemn him so blindly. And, if he had taken her out, he had never promised her anything or actually asked for anything in return but a few kisses. Now, because of her own impetuousness, she acknowledged that there could be no renewal of even the friendship between them, for she knew he would never be prepared to overlook the things she had said.

She hadn't really expected to hear from Guy again, although he had said he would see her in the morning. He had spoken in the heat of the moment and she hadn't taken him seriously. When he did send for her she was startled, but as her surprise faded a little, she felt a flicker of new hope. Would he treat her more gently than he had done a few hours ago? If he showed even the smallest signs of relenting, she must be willing to meet him halfway. She forgot all about the pitfalls of being friends with him as she decided feverishly that a few crumbs would be better than no bread at all.

Not having been to his office before, she was forced to ask the maid who brought the message with her breakfast where it was. Each morning her breakfast was brought to her suite. Often she only wanted coffee and toast, but she revelled in the unaccustomed luxury. This morning she was up when it arrived and the girl who brought it set it out on the table in Alana's lounge while she relayed Guy's message.

'You'll find it just along the passage from the manager's office.' The girl glanced at Alana quickly. 'It's on the ground floor.'

Guy had asked her to be there at eleven and she turned up five minutes early. The glamorous young woman whom she rightly guessed to be his temporary secretary smiled at her politely and asked her to wait. Having to wait started her off trembling again as her earlier optimism diminished and she wondered just what was in store for her.

Last night, or rather, early this morning, Guy had made it quite clear that she was to stay until she had repaid the loan. Probably he intended asking her to sign a document or something to that effect, just to make sure that she did.

When at last she was summoned to his presence, he was ready for her. Half expecting to find him still occupied with business, in order to make her wait even longer, Alana was surprised to find him leaning back in his chair, arms folded, watching her enter his office without any expression on his face.

He's good at that, she thought, with an involuntary shiver. When he chose he could be so sphinx-like she would defy anyone to know what he was thinking.

When he motioned for her to sit down her legs felt so weak she was glad to do so. He was like a stranger, cool and remote, and she didn't know what to say to him. Unhappily she began wondering how she would ever manage without his warm teasing companionship. Even if she hadn't discovered who he was it might not have lasted, but while it had it had been very pleasant. Now it was gone she knew an incredible sense of loss. And, despite her tentative hopes, she guessed it had gone for ever.

'Well, Miss Hurst,' he waited for her to be seated, then began, 'I've spent some time this morning looking into your affairs, and, so far as I can see, everything's in order. You signed a contract in which you agreed to sing for us for six months, unless the management agrees to release you. After six months it will become subject for renewal, providing both sides wishes to continue.'

'I know all that,' she broke in, her face paling before his renewed coldness. 'I realise that apart from the money you might not have been willing to release me.'

'You did say you wanted to leave.' As if to remind her of the exact moment he drew contemplative fingers across the still red scratch on his cheek. 'Consequently, in view of your slightly unstable tendencies, I considered it made sense to bring you here and make sure you understand that under no circumstances will we agree to letting you go.'

Alana tried not to dwell on the insults he was handing out, for fear it made her angry again. When no anger managed to penetrate her deep depression, she glanced humbly at him and said desperately, 'I'm sorry I was so hasty last night, Guy . . .'

'I think,' he advised silkily, ignoring her abject apology, much in the same way as she had ignored his, 'I think it might be better if you used my proper name from now on. I'm sure you'll find it no hardship, last night you seemed inordinately fond of it.'

About to protest, she hesitated, her eyes darkening miserably. Was there any use in saying anything? She suddenly doubted if anything could ever put things right between them, and perhaps it was just as well. To be enemies rather than friends might make life more bearable in the long run than the other way round. Feeling as she did about Guy, it would be wiser to see as little as possible of him in future, and to think of him as Mr Renwich might help her to forget.

'Just as you like, Mr Renwick,' she said gravely, lifting her chin slightly, as though unconsciously trying to prove she had a little pride left.

'Good!' He continued to look coldly satisfied. 'Now, can we come to your room—as you wish all our future dealings to be on a strictly businesslike footing.'

'If I'm to stay——' she began, 'I mean,' she corrected herself hastily, 'as I'm staying, I don't mind remaining where I am. If I spoke of my rooms disparagingly, I'm sorry. They're really very nice.'

'Well, just as you like,' he agreed suavely. 'Naturally, of course, we shall have to charge you for the accommodation. It can come off your salary.'

Alana felt her heart beating over quickly with apprehension. She hadn't thought of this? 'How—how much?' she stammered, her eyes fixed anxiously on his.

'I believe we could let you have it at a considerable reduction. Say, a hundred pounds a week?'

A hundred pounds a week! Alana went so cold she feared he might see her shivering. A hundred pounds was almost as much as she earned in a week, and he must know it. Oh, how could he? Quite easily, an inner voice answered her. And hadn't she brought most of this on herself? Well, almost, she admitted bitterly, but did Guy Renwick never make allowances for human frailty? This morning his voice was cool and clipped, his eyes icy hard and unforgiving. He was a stranger and intended remaining one, and there didn't seem a thing she could do about it.

'I can't afford that much,' she whispered bleakly. 'I'd better look round for something outside.' She could never go back to Mrs Brice, but there must be other places.

'I thought you might find it a little more than you could manage,' he said sardonically, 'but I'm sure we can find you something else. Not that we have a lot of more modest accommodation, I'm afraid. You probably imagine the terms I quoted were exorbitant, but I can assure you, for a suite like the one you're occupying, in London, I could get much more.'

If he assured her of one other thing, she would scream! 'I'm sure you're right,' she agreed hollowly.

His eyes rested on her white, strained face with a

cold flash of triumph. 'You can be,' he said smoothly. 'However, it wouldn't be convenient to have you living out of the hotel, so if I arrange for you to have something around, say, twenty pounds a week, would that suit you better?'

'Yes,' she said, trying to look happier and wondering why she didn't feel it. Guy was watching her speculatively and she didn't trust the gleam in his eyes. He smiled, and his smile had the sort of hardness she'd never seen before.

'I'll arrange for you to eat in the staff dining-room,' he told her. 'You can, of course, if you like, eat out— your little sandwich bar around the corner perhaps. But if you prefer it, I can easily add full board to the cost of your room, and it might be cheaper.'

Would she ever be able to eat or sleep again? But, if she had to, did it matter where? Silently she nodded, scrambling to her feet as she muttered a few incoherent words of thanks. She was terrified, if she stayed any longer, that she might disgrace herself by bursting into tears. 'If that's all, Mr Renwick?'

'All for the moment,' he said unpleasantly, making no attempt to rise to his own feet, which left Alana in little doubt as to the exact amount of respect he accorded her. 'You may go now, but I shall send for you in a day or two, after I get a legal document drawn up for you to sign, regarding the money you—er— borrowed from me.'

Why didn't hee say, the money you tried to steal, and be done with it! Hateful creature! she gasped, hurrying towards her suite, then hesitating. If she went there she might only indulge in the tears it was taking her all her time to suppress. And she had to get away from that insolent man with whom she had just spent one of the worst half hours in her life! Her suite wouldn't be far enough!

Rushing from the hotel, she went to the park. There

were quite a lot of people there, strolling happily in the early spring sunshine. She thought she would never find a quiet spot, but at last she did. The secluded seat behind a clump of thick bushes was empty and she sat very still, praying no one would come near until she had herself under control. Guy's ruthlessness had left her physically shaken, but she dared not contemplate the state of her heart. A tear escaped, rolling down her cheek, and desperately she brushed it away. If Guy could see her now, she thought, his triumph would be complete!

Someone came and sat beside her and she glanced up in dismay. It was Fabian Marlow, the last person she expected to see. 'Oh, hello,' she murmured.

'Can I be of any help?' he asked gently. 'I noticed you leave the hotel and you seemed distracted. That's why I followed you here.'

'It's nothing. I had a headache.' She managed a weak smile, hoping her poor head would forgive all the headaches she'd invented lately.

'Nevertheless,' said Fabian, his eyes on her pale, tear-stained face, 'I think I'll leave my shoulder where it is for a few minutes, just in case you need it.'

Fabian was nice. He had a warm, comforting effect on her. In his company she never found it difficult to relax. He was always interested, but he never probed. Nor did he expect her to be without a fault, as Guy apparently did! And, if there was something he didn't approve of, she was sure Fabian would make allowances, as Guy did not. Why couldn't Guy have been more like him? she wondered later, as he escorted her back to the Remax. They had talked and he had bought her a cup of coffee, and she felt a lot better, and very grateful.

'I have to be away for the next couple of nights,' Fabian frowned, looking as if he wished he hadn't to go away at all. 'Maybe we can meet for a drink, though, as soon as I return.'

Alana agreed, then they parted and she went up to her suite. The cleaners were in and she apologised. 'I'll wait,' she smiled.

There were two of them and they glanced at each other with a trace of embarrassment. 'I'm sorry, Miss Hurst,' said one, fiddling uncomfortably with the duster she was holding, 'I'm afraid the suite's empty. We had orders to take your things up to room 504, that's on the next floor, but we were told you knew about it.'

'Oh, yes of course,' Alana assured the woman hastily, 'but I expected to have to do it myself, so it's a pleasant surprise.'

Whether or not they believed her, she didn't really care. A surge of bitterness and humiliation almost overwhelmed her. She had agreed to move, but had imagined Guy would give her a few days, not move her out immediately, as if there was a fire! He certainly wasn't going to let her think he might relent and change his mind. Nor was he apparently giving himself a chance to do so. She could see by the curious glances the cleaning ladies were giving her that they were wondering what was going on. Well, let them wonder, she thought defiantly.

Swiftly she went over the lounge to what had been her bedroom. Quickly she opened each drawer, but every one was empty, even her personal belongings had been removed. How could Guy do this to her? she fumed, while she hid her hurt from the cleaning ladies and murmured, 'Just checking.'

Room 504 was adequate, but only just. There she found all her things, as the ladies had promised. At least, her suitcases were there, but they hadn't been unpacked for her—another indication, she thought wryly, of her changed status! The room was comfortable, but a far cry from the suite she had just vacated. A carpet, of disputable age, covered the floor and there was a small wardrobe and dressing-table and a single bed. In one corner was a basin and two taps, but no bathroom or shower. She must remember to find out if these facilities were far along the corridor. She surveyed it a moment with a frown; she had seen worse, she would survive. It wasn't the room she minded so much as the speculation it would cause. If only Guy had sent her up here when she had first arrived, how much easier it would have been.

It took some time to transfer her clothes from the cases to their respective drawers and hangers. She noted with dismay that the women hadn't packed them very carefully and already some of her new dresses were very creased. When she finished she saw it was well after two and Milo was expecting her before three for a rehearsal. He had two new numbers he wanted her to try out.

Owing to having to change rooms in such a hurry, Alana had forgotten all about lunch. Now she wouldn't have time for it, but it didn't matter, she didn't feel particularly hungry. On her way down in the lift, she decided she would eat out, rather than use the staff dining-room, if for no other reason than that it might be cheaper. Guy had said he would give her a price for full board, but she suspected it might be more than she cared to pay. If she could find some place cheaper outside it would mean there would be more money to send home for her parents.

She found one of her new numbers extremely difficult, and Milo lost his patience several times before she was able to sing it in a way that pleased him. It was a haunting little song about a girl who had been rejected by her lover, and she didn't want Milo to see how the poignancy of it brought sweat to her brow. It reminded her too much of what had just taken place between Guy and herself and, although he hadn't been her lover, she had loved him.

When eventually she began singing with confidence, Milo smiled with relief. Then she turned her head and saw Guy watching her, and her voice faded completely.

While Milo pretended to tear out his hair, she began trembling. 'I—I forgot the line,' she stammered, her face white as the band wailed to a stop and someone played a mocking little ha-ha on a fiddle.

Guy had a nerve to turn up and watch her as usual! Alana would liked to have glared at him, but somehow couldn't find the courage to look at him any way at all. 'I'm sorry,' she apologised to Milo. 'Shall I begin again?'

Milo stopped abusing his not over-luxuriant hair to study her thoughtfully. 'Did you have any lunch today, darling?'

She wasn't deceived by the habitual endearment and didn't dare lie. 'I had some coffee,' she didn't say when.

'I thought as much,' he said sharply, as Guy came nearer. 'See that you have more than a cup of coffee in future.'

Nodding numbly, she was frozen by the coldness in Guy's eyes as they caught and held her own. Whatever his reason for being here, it certainly wasn't to forgive her. His face was still as hard as it had been that morning.

'Do you want me to try again?' she repeated anxiously.

'No!' Milo surprised her by throwing a protective arm around her slender shoulders and, ignoring Guy, kissed her lightly on the brow. 'You'll have to do better tonight, though,' he teased, 'or I'll sack you!'

Alana felt a bubble of hysterical laughter rise to her throat as Guy's mouth tightened. 'Mr Renwick,' she choked, suddenly finding it terribly funny, 'absolutely refuses to sack me.'

Guy's face bore a tight, cruel, you'll-pay-for-this expression. 'I can always find you something else, Miss Hurst. In the domestic line, perhaps?'

As no one seemed to know whether to treat this as a joke or not, Alana said quickly, 'I promise I'll have it off pat before I go on this evening, Milo.' She ignored Guy's remark but knew she wouldn't forget it. As she muttered a hurried excuse and left, the threat in his voice and eyes seemed to follow her.

On the top floor, in her room, she lay on her bed thinking how foolish she had been to provoke him. She would be the one to suffer. Remembering the coldness of his eyes as she departed, she shivered. Because of the contract she had signed and the money she had borrowed from him, she must be completely at his mercy.

CHAPTER SIX

THAT evening when Alana came back to sing for the last time she was dismayed to find Guy sitting at his usual table, which must obviously be kept reserved for him. Unhappyily she wished he wouldn't stare at her so. Then she realised bitterly why he was doing it. He hoped to put her off her stride, to cause her to make a mistake he could criticise. His dark gaze burning into her almost succeeded in doing this, but not quite. Somehow she manged to hang on to her sanity. There was one disturbing moment, though, worse than the rest. In the middle of her sad little number, their eyes met and clung, and for several long seconds they seemed to be completely alone.

Someone moved between them, or it may have been

a flicker of the lights, but it mercifully gave her a chance to pull herself together. She didn't look at him again, not even when she finished singing and received wildly enthusiastic applause. If there was anything in his eyes now it would only be mockery, she suspected.

'They're coming to like you,' Milo teased, putting an arm round her waist and bowing as he shared the limelight. 'I thought they might.'

Glancing down at the deep cleavage of her dress, Alana blushed. 'I know what they like,' she retorted dryly, and Milo laughed.

The next night, when her glance was helplessly drawn to the spot where, until now, Guy had sat alone, she received a distinct shock. He was there, but he had a woman with him, a very sophisticated, redhaired beauty. Alana's eyes widened as she gazed at them, and, as if becoming conscious of her intent appraisal, he turned his head in her direction. Even from a distance Alana felt a shaft of flame running through her and she wondered desperately if there was no way she could escape his strong attraction. Then the woman at his side claimed his attention and Alana swallowed hard as she saw the charming smile he bestowed on her.

It was after midnight when Milo whispered in her ear, 'The boss wants a word with you, darling.'

She hadn't discussed Guy's deception with Milo. She had merely told him she had discovered who Guy really was and left it at that. Milo had glanced at her keenly and merely shrugged and said he had thought that eventually she would. He had made no further comment or offered any apology for his part in the affair.

Now, after he had delivered Guy's message, she looked at him anxiously, more than a trace of apprehension in her vivid blue eyes. 'Couldn't you tell him I'm too busy, Milo?'

'I'm afraid not,' he sighed.

She approached Guy and his lady-friend reluctantly, her stomach in knots, wondering if this was the woman Fabian had told her about, the Veronica Templeton with whom he had spent the weekend at his cottage.

'Mrs Templeton expressed a wish to meet you,' Guy said stiffly, when she reached them, immediately confirming her suspicions. As she shivered involuntarily, his eyes went insolently over her. 'Another time when I send for you, Miss Hurst, don't take so long in getting here.'

'I enjoyed your singing very much, Miss Hurst,' Veronica Templeton intervened warmly. 'I like your voice, it suits my ears.'

Which must be a compliment of a sort. Uncertainly Alana murmured a word of thanks, trying to infuse a little warmth into the voice Mrs Templeton professed to admire. It didn't help to reduce her despair to note that at close quarters Mrs Templeton was even more attractive than she had first appeared to be. She was pleasant and friendly, too. Alana could find no obvious fault, and her heart sank. It stood out a mile that she would make Guy Mason Renwick a very suitable wife, and that he appeared to think so.

As Guy politely pulled out a chair for her and she sat down, Veronica gushed on, 'I do so admire your dress.'

'What there is of it,' Guy added derisively, his mouth tightening.

'Guy has a cousin whose sole ambition was to be a singer,' Veronica continued, as though to explain his attitude. 'Of course even a year or two ago it was considered more risqué than it is now and her father put his foot down. Does she still hanker after such a bizarre career, darling?' she asked sweetly of Guy.

Not quite without claws? Alana decided wryly.

'I think she's going to settle for marriage and raising

a family,' Guy replied coolly, 'which I believe will suit her much better.'

'Oh, do you think so?' Veronica's voice was unmistakably eager, while her eyes were melting.

Guy said tersely, 'I wouldn't like to think of Jane doing anything like this, anyway.'

Alana felt a hot flush rising to her cheeks. He wasn't even attempting to veil his insults! Well, she wasn't going to sit here and let them make a meal of her! Nor did she intend protesting that singing was as respectable as anything else—as the glint in Guy's eye hinted he expected her to. 'If you'll excuse me?' she murmured instead, preparing to leave.

'Oh, you can't go yet!' Veronica cried. 'Guy darling, you haven't asked her about the party!'

'You ask her,' he shrugged, his eyes fixed on Alana's hot face. 'It was your idea.'

Veronica laughed charmingly. 'Guy's giving a little party next week, to celebrate something, I believe,' she cast him a coy glance, 'and I thought it would be nice if you would come along and sing, perhaps something appropriate for a newly engaged couple?'

Engaged couple? So Fabian was right, after all! Alana knew she had gone pale, but she had suffered so much, one way and another, over the past few weeks, she had grown adept at hiding her feelings. This last shock was worse than the others she had received and she was aware of Veronica looking at her curiously.

Veronica smiled as she caught her eye. 'Guy will arrange for you to have the night off, if that's why you're hesitating.'

'Naturally, that will be no problem,' Guy drawled, his voice edged with a sudden hard satisfaction. 'I'm sure, darling,' to Veronica, 'Miss Hurst won't let us down.'

'No, of course not,' Alana agreed, then left them with a brief word of farewell, knowing she couldn't stay another minute. She had no intention of going to their engagement party; she would think of an excuse, even if it meant inventing laryngitis! If this was Guy's way of ensuring the complete destruction of any rosy dreams she still cherished about him, he had certainly succeeded!

It was during the next afternoon, when she was resting, that he came to see her. She hadn't gone down to practise. Milo had another singer to interview and had told Alana she could take the afternoon off. Alana knew Milo liked to have at least two other girls he could call on in an emergency, so she wasn't worried about her own position.

She did, in fact, welcome having the afternoon off as she had slept badly and gone out early to do some necessary shopping and she felt tired.

Having just had a shower, in the bathroom she had found at the other end of the corridor, she was lying on her bed, sleepily relaxed, when Guy walked in. She had no warning. One moment the room was quiet and empty with only the sound of the wind, for the afternoon had grown stormy, and the distant hum of traffic, the next moment he was there, looming above her.

'How did you get in?' she gasped, sitting up with a start.

'I have a master key,' he said, quite unrepentantly.

'Well, don't use it again,' she snapped, making a rather muddled attempt to pull her robe around her and to restore some order to her tumbled hair. Her lips came together in a straight line. He was contemptible! How could he be so callous, so insensitive as to come here? If he had to come, why didn't he just state his business and go? Not that she was all that keen to hear what he had to say, because she was sure it wouldn't be pleasant. Beneath his cynical gaze she felt trapped, for there wasn't anywhere she could go to get properly dressed.

A remorseless smile touched his lips as he stood in the doorway watching her helpless attempts to wrap her arms around her quivering body. Her thick, shining hair fell over her shoulders while loose strands of it curled over her heaving breast. 'Why so angry?' he asked smoothly.

'Haven't I a right to be?' she retorted, as his eyes roamed boldly over her.

'I'd stop stressing my rights, if I were you,' he advised silkily. 'It's not a habit you can afford.'

How could one man arouse so much anger? She could have killed him, and not for the first time. 'What do you want?' she asked rudely, glaring at him.

Stepping over the threshold, he closed the door. 'In my official capacity as hotel proprietor,' he replied sarcastically, 'perhaps I came to see if you were satisfied with your new room.'

'I like it better when you aren't in it,' she answered fiercely.

'You do?' his smile was mocking. 'You're ready to admit I make a difference?'

While counting ten, she noticed the way her heart was behaving and decided it might be wiser to concentrate on getting rid of him, rather than continue fighting him. An icy finger traced a cold path down her spine. Whatever happened he must never guess how she felt about him.

'You surely didn't come all the way up here just to assure yourself of my comfort, Mr Renwick?'

'It's not exactly Everest,' he said dryly. 'Two seconds in the lift from the ground floor and about the same on foot from my apartment on the floor below.'

Alana's dark lashes fluttered. Did he have to make that sound like a threat? If his rooms were directly under hers, only a thin ceiling would divide them at night. Was he deliberately making sure she was aware of it?

When a slight obstruction in her throat kept her silent, he added, 'I did bring a paper for you to sign, but there's no hurry.'

There was all the hurry in the world, and she knew what it was. 'I'll sign now,' she snapped, biting her lip with impatience when he didn't immediately produce it.

While she gripped her hands tightly together in agitation, he prowled towards her dressing-table where she had deposited the tin of dried milk and packet of biscuits which she had bought that morning. The hotel provided tea-making facilities in the shape of teabags and a kettle, so it would be quite easy to make her own breakfast.

She watched Guy as he stood, lean and tall in his usual dark pants and shirt, reading the name on the packet of biscuits. 'You don't eat in the hotel?' he rapped suddenly. 'Why not?'

If she told him to mind his own damned business, as she felt like doing, he would only persist. 'Because I like going out,' she said mutinously.

He turned to look at her steadily, a hint of colour running under his cheeks. 'You came in today with Fabian Marlow. I didn't know you were acquainted.'

'A lot of men speak to me, Mr Renwick,' she taunted. 'It happens to bizarre night club singers.'

He gave no indication of being aware of her jibe, although his eyes went glacial. 'You attract a lot of attention, I've noticed.'

'You aren't accusing me of seeking it deliberately, Mr Renwick?'

His voice began matching his eyes. 'That dress you were wearing last night, Miss Hurst, was almost indecently suggestive. When we left you the freedom to choose your own wardrobe I imagined you would use more discretion.'

Recalling how he had stared at her as she had sat at

his table, she went hot with rage and resentment. 'You may have thought you'd given me the freedom of choice,' she all but spat, 'but in actual fact I had none.'

'Then go back tomorrow and get something else,' he snapped. 'I refuse to have my employees going round half naked.'

'Some of your guests aren't much better!'

'I'm not talking about my guests, if that's what you like to call them. They can wear what the hell they like and good luck to them. But not you, so don't argue, just do as I say!'

Averting her confused gaze, Alana thought she would never understand him. Milo's other girls often wore much less than she did and no one appeared to raise any objections. Of course, since they had quarrelled Guy had never missed an opportunity of humiliating her. This was obviously what he was trying to do now, and some men, when they thought they had a girl at their mercy, became sadists.

'I'll think about it,' she murmured coolly, then, hoping to get rid of him before she burst into tears, 'Won't Mrs Templeton be waiting?'

'She isn't my keeper.'

'I'll admit the collar and lead isn't visible,' Alana choked, 'but I'm sure she wouldn't approve of you being here.'

'Oh,' he drawled insolently, 'she doesn't mind my little diversions.'

Something exploded in Alana's head. Furiously she glared at him. 'I wouldn't be one of those for all the tea in China!'

'Wouldn't you, Miss Hurst?' he smiled, his smile that of a predatory tiger as he came, silent-footed, to drop down beside her.

As the bed creaked beneath his weight, she stared at him, momentarily stunned into immobility. His insolence was beyond belief! She would have her revenge somehow, she thought, as he stared back at her and the tiny, familiar shock waves began rippling down her spine. And, if it took a hundred years, she would prove to him he didn't affect her in the slightest.

His gaze narrowed on her face, his dark eyes seeming to be touching each feature but not halting until they came to her mouth, where the softening contours unconsciously betrayed her. He couldn't be debating whether to kiss her or not, surely? He was a devil, she sensed an angry one, for all he tried to hide it. He could be trying to decide how he could hurt her most.

It didn't make sense that one part of her craved for the feel of his mouth on hers while the other half rejected it. Her fevered awareness of the intention she read in his eyes was balanced by her mounting resistance to it. On no account must she give in and allow him to believe she might be putty in his hands. Putty which he could mould and do exactly what he liked with.

The brush of his lips against hers had her nerves tensing with shock, but he didn't wait for her to protest. He only waited until she got as far as opening her mouth before smothering her choked cry with the increasing pressure of his. The feeling this aroused was instant and dramatic. It brought a searing storm of sensation racing through her body and complete devastation to her mind. Before she knew what was happening he had eased her back and they were lying flat on the bed, Guy crushing her to him, his mouth pulverising hers, while his hands roughly tore the robe from her shaking limbs.

Her stomach was churning, her heart rocketing. Whichever way he did it, wherever it was, how did he manage to fill her with such wild delight? Desire raced through her veins as he held her tightly, her pleasure being such that no breath of shame or regret could sweep it away. Her arms went feverishly around his neck, a gesture, she realised weakly, which must speak louder than words. She tried to speak but her heart was knocking crazily against her ribs and her breath coming, when he allowed it, in shaky gasps. If she had never been frightened of her own emotions before, Alana knew she was now.

It seemed to go on for a long time, his mouth taking hers by storm, moving insidiously over her, while something between them, volcanic and dangerous, threatened the last of her defences. He didn't attempt to conceal his sensual hunger and a wave of deep longing swept over her, so powerful as to be inescapable. Helplessly she clung to him, increasing his already mounting passion by doing so, but unable to deny the tumultuous force of her own response. She went curiously boneless as with a frustrated groan he moulded her to his hard male strength.

He wanted her, she could feel it, and suddenly she didn't want to refuse him anything. She must have hurt him terribly with her hysterical accusations. It must be up to her to put things right. And if this was the only way to do it, had she any other choice? After all, didn't she love him?

As his mouth lifted slightly, she moved her bruised lips. 'Guy,' she whispered, 'won't you forgive me for what I said the other night? If you care for me, I'm willing to prove how sorry I am.'

'Care for you!' As if her words brought him swiftly back to reality, he pulled savagely away from her, 'You have an outsize opinion of yourself if you think I could ever care for a girl like you!'

'Please, Guy!' she pleaded, her face paling as his anger struck her harshly.

'Save it,' he snapped, refusing to listen, his eyes black, burning holes in his face. 'You use every trick in the book, don't you? But I don't want your sort and never will.'

As she shrank back, the blood beating in her ears
nearly deafened her, but she thought she heard him
cursing tersely, something about needing his brains
examined for getting involved with such a cheap little
cheat. For a moment he paused, after buttoning his
shirt and tucking it in. But it was only a moment.
Then, with another stifled exclamation, he was gone,
so swiftly she thought he might have been a ghost.

Unhappy enough after her disturbing confrontation
with Guy, Alana felt she could well have done without
the additional despair which a letter from her mother
brought. Her parents asked for more money. They had
almost decided to sell the house, her mother wrote.
And if they did they should soon be able to repay her.
However, the estate agent they had approached wasn't
able to promise they would get rid of such a huge
property very quickly, and for this same reason their
bank manager wouldn't allow them to increase their
overdraft, so it was imperative that Alana sent them
something to tide them over. Everyone knew actresses
made a lot of money. If they hadn't spent so much on
her education, Mrs Hurst funished reproachfully, they
might have had something put aside for a rainy day.

Tearing the letter up in tiny pieces, Alana threw it
in her waste-paper basket. What on earth was she to
do? she asked herself unsteadily. Her mother appeared
to imagine she was an actress, making a fortune. It was
the same old story—creditors pressing for payment.
The agent and bank manager had a right to be dubious.
Who wanted a ten-bedroomed house today? They
probably hadn't a hope of getting rid of it.

Brooding on the edge of desperation, she filled the
hotel kettle and plugged it in, hoping a cup of tea might
help her to think of something. But before it had time
to boil, Guy's secretary rang, saying he wanted to see
her immediately. With a sigh she switched the kettle

off and glanced at her watch. It was still early. She fancied she knew what he wanted to see her about, but need he be in such a hurry? Her mother's letter had left her feeling terribly distraught, and she could have done without another interview with Guy this morning.

When she arrived at his office it was just after nine. 'You forgot to sign our agreement yesterday,' he said curtly, as she walked in.

'You didn't produce it, Mr Renwick.' She strove to sound flippant, wishing her heart wouldn't begin performing acrobatics every time she saw him. This morning he looked well, much fitter, she felt sure, than she did. Beside him, in a pair of old jeans and shirt, she felt positively scruffy, and wondered wistfully when she would ever be able to afford some new clothes.

'I allowed myself to be diverted,' he replied with bored cynicism, rounding off his own tour of inspection coolly, 'but it won't happen again.'

'I'm glad,' she agreed with emphasis, even managing a taunting smile. 'Now, if you'll kindly give me the document you've had drawn up, I'll sign it. Then I can forget all about it.'

In her anxiety to hide her hurt, she appeared to have overdone it. As livid anger leapt to his face, she thought he was about to explode and braced herself. 'You seem to have no sense of remorse, Miss Hurst,' he rasped. 'When you repay what you owe you can forget it, not before. I presume,' he queried sharply, 'you've used this money to pay off your debts?'

'Yes,' she whispered, averting her glance.

'What exactly were they, might I ask?'

'No—I mean, I'm sorry. You have no right,' she cried, fright making her answer sound far more belligerent than she had intended it to be. She was aching to confide in him, but she had promised her parents. 'I can't,' she muttered miserably.

Guy didn't appear to notice her unhappiness. Leaving his desk, he towered over her. He hadn't asked her to sit down. 'People often amaze me!' he snapped. 'They grovel when they want something, but as soon as they have it they do their best to make you believe they've done you a favour.'

'Perhaps it's a natural enough reaction,' she choked. 'It's never easy to beg. I hated borrowing from you.'

'Don't worry,' he retorted grimly, 'I'd certainly never loan you anything again.'

'You won't be asked to,' she assured him bleakly.

'Nor will you ask anyone else!' he rapped imperiously, his grey eyes icy.

'You don't run my whole life!' she gasped, her face white.

'Not yet.'

Before she could think of a suitable reply to that, his secretary buzzed him.

'Yes?' he snapped. After the girl relayed her message, he controlled his impatience and spoke in quieter tones. 'That will be fine, Miss Smith. Please ask her to wait. I won't be long.'

No sooner had he turned from the intercom, however, than the door opened and Veronica Templeton sailed in.

'Oh, I'm so sorry, darling,' she apologised prettily when she saw Alana, 'I didn't know you had company. Your secretary did you say you were engaged, but all good secretaries say that. I thought you were just working.'

Guy glanced at her quickly, then accepted her apology with a dry smile. 'That's quite all right, Veronica. Do come in. Miss Hurst was just leaving.'

After staring at him for a brief moment, Alana turned away. If the warmth of his smile was a trifle forced, it was she whom he dismissed, not Veronica.

And, as she went out, she found herself again tortured
by the sight of them standing closely together. Guy's
face had relaxed, he looked altogether changed. He
hadn't been able to get rid of her quickly enough, she
realised.

But not even Guy could command all her thoughts
that morning as the more urgent matter of another loan
for her mother preyed on Alana's mind. She could
never approach Guy again, even if he had been willing,
which he definitely was not. Then, as she returned to
her room, she suddenly thought of Fabian Marlow and
wondered if she dared approach him.

Without giving herself time to think it over, as if
subconsciously aware this would spell death to such an
idea, she reached quickly for a pen and paper. She
would ask Fabian to help her out. Hadn't he once said
he was a millionaire? If he was, he wouldn't miss a
thousand pounds. He might be willing to let her have
it, especially if she was able to convince him there was
every likelihood of it being repaid in the near future.

Despite her attempts to consider this as a purely
business transaction, a few minutes later Alana viewed
the note she had written with total distaste. If her
mother could have guessed what this was costing her
daughter in terms of real hurt and embarrassment,
Alana was sure she would never have asked her for
anything. If only Andrew was here, she thought wistfully.

But Andrew wasn't. His wife was still ill and Alana
knew she couldn't just stand by while their parents
went to prison. Did it matter how much she suffered,
if she could save them? Once the house was sold there
should be no more problems. She would explain how
she was only receiving a modest salary and they would
soon settle up with Guy and Fabian.

Sealing her note in an envelope, she took it down to
reception, asking one of the girls on duty to see that

Mr Marlow received it. She decided to do it this way, rather than approach him personally, for if he was reluctant to loan her anything, he might find it easier to send her a note in return, rather than refuse her request to her face.

As she hurried away, she failed to notice the tall figure hovering in the doorway of the inner office. Nor did she see him grimly reading the address on the letter she left, with a dark frown on his face.

Fabian sent for her, scarcely half an hour later. She was surprised he had got her letter so quickly but relieved as well, for the waiting in her room had become so intolerable she wasn't able to sit still. Having thought of going out for a while to try and relieve her increasing agitation, she didn't even stop to throw off the jacket she had put on. That Fabian had sent for her must be a good sign and it seemed more important to see him as soon as possible.

His suite, where she hadn't been before, was proof that he hadn't been boasting when he had talked of being wealthy. The sheer luxury of it almost took her breath away, or might have done if she hadn't been so obsessed by her worries.

Taking her to the lounge, he asked her to sit down. Doing as she was told, Alana glanced at him anxiously. He didn't smile, but neither did he look terribly discouraging.

'This is nice,' she commented, feeling it was a rather inane remark to make, considering why she was here, but she was so nervous she couldn't think of anything better. Making an effort, she asked, 'Do you live here all the time——'

'Mostly I'm in America.' Fabian stared at her closely as he sat down beside her. 'So it's easier to stay here when I have to visit London.'

'I see.' Feeling suddenly faint, she closed her eyes tightly.

'Alana honey, relax! I got your note—if that's what's bothering you.' His brow creased in a wry smile. 'It's a bit unusual, but nothing, I'm sure, to get so worked up about.'

'I didn't enjoy asking you for money, Fabian.' Tensely she looked at him again, trying to hide her distress. 'I only want a loan, but all the same, I didn't find it easy to approach you. I wouldn't have asked you for a penny if I hadn't good reason to believe it will be all repaid with interest in a month or two.'

Without speaking he rose to his feet again, but it was only to get her a drink. Gently he placed it in her hands before resuming his seat. 'Drink it up,' he said firmly as she hesitated. 'You seem in need of it.' While she dazedly obeyed him, he drained his own glass. 'I needed mine too,' he explained enigmatically.

Alana drew a confused breath. 'If you're worried about the repayments, I promise you'll . . .'

'It's not that,' he cut in sharply, before she could finish. 'I don't give a damn about the money. You can have it and I don't want it back. But I do want you!'

'Oh, no!' Completely startled, she jumped up, her blue eyes wide with dismay.

'Please, honey!' He was on his feet almost as quickly as she was. 'It's not what you think, or what you seem to be thinking. I'm not asking you to have an affair. I want to marry you.'

'Marry me?' she gasped.

'I love you,' he insisted urgently. 'I believe we could be very happy together.'

Alana's legs suddenly gave way beneath her, forcing her to sit down again. This couldn't be happening to her! Fabian was nice and she liked him, but she was sure she had never given him any reason to believe her feelings towards him were any warmer than that. She was more stunned than ever when he confessed:

'I'd better tell you I was engaged to another girl. At

least, we were about to announce our engagement when I met you and realised I couldn't go through with it. I rang and told her about five minutes ago.'

'But I haven't agreed to anything!' Alana stammered wildly. 'You hadn't asked. You should have waited!'

'It doesn't matter,' Fabian muttered stubbornly. 'Whatever your decision, I'd be no use to her now. Besides, she sounded so hysterical when I spoke to her that I doubt if she'll ever forgive me.'

Alana strove to control her own rising hysteria. 'You're a fool, Fabian,' she cried hoarsely. 'How do you know that you love me? A lot of men fall for the glamour of a night club singer, but it's often not real. Under all the glitter we're just ordinary girls. I am, anyway,' she assured him feverishly.

'There's nothing artificial about you this morning,' he countered flatly. 'I don't believe you are wearing a scrap of make-up. And your clothes,' he added frankly, 'are far from glamorous. Yet you're still the loveliest little thing I've ever seen.'

Wincing at his exaggerated turn of phrase, Alana stared at him desperately. She was sure Fabian was only infatuated and would soon come to his senses, but what could she say to convince him? This poor girl he'd been engaged to, what must she be going through?

'I can't believe you would so callously end your engagement,' she whispered incredulously.

At her continuing disapproval, Fabian became as sulky as a small boy. 'Well, whether you believe it or not, it's a fact, and I'm making you a deal. Marry me and you can have all the money you want, otherwise you don't get a penny.'

Alana felt herself tremble. One wouldn't have to be a great judge of character to be able to detect the flaw in Fabian's. He'd made his millions and believed they could buy him anything he desired. Yet somehow, he didn't seem so spoiled as unhappy. His eyes were tormented as he stared down on her, and she suddenly feared he had developed some kind of fondness for her and meant what he said.

'I'll have to have time to think,' she muttered distractedly, meaning she would have to have time to try and find some other way of raising the money. She couldn't possibly consider Fabian's proposal, not feeling as she did about Guy. It would have to be a last resort. Even then she didn't think she could do it.

Minutes later, having told him she would let him know her decision as soon as possible, she left the hotel. But although for the next few hours she tramped London, she was no nearer to finding a solution to her problems at the end of them. No reputable firm, it seemed, was willing to advance her anything without some form of security, while the disreputable ones, as she chose to call them, demanded exorbitant interest.

Trying to swallow the cup of coffee she eventually bought herself, Alana wondered what to do next. Whatever happened she couldn't marry Fabian: that much was clear. And she must find him as soon as possible and tell him so. Guiltily she realised she should have been more emphatic about this before she came out. It had been foolish of her to leave him so obviously hopeful.

It was almost three when she hurried back to the Remax, but as she entered the hotel a receptionist called her. There was an urgent message from Milo. He wanted to see her immediately she came in. Wondering anxiously what it could be about, Alana went straight to his office. She would have to see Fabian later, she decided. Milo wouldn't have sent for her if it had merely been something trivial, she was sure.

He was talking to someone on the telephone when she found him, but as soon as she came in he dropped the receiver and told her to take a seat. As she did so she thought he was acting rather strangely. He glanced at her quickly, then away again, while running a nervous hand around the back of his neck. She got the feeling he had something to say but didn't know where to begin.

Because Milo was seldom hesitant, she felt a flicker of alarm. 'What is it?' she asked at last, when she could bear his silence no longer. 'Is it bad news? Has Mr Renwick asked you to get rid of me or something?' Guy had said she must stay, but he could have changed his mind.

'No, nothing like that,' Milo exclaimed, then sighed, 'Not quite like that, anyway.'

While he still hesitated, Alana said uneasily, 'You sent for me and said it was urgent, so I wish you would tell me what it is and be done with it. Nothing could be much worse than sitting here, trying to guess.'

'You're right. I'm sorry,' Milo shot her another quick glance. 'It's difficult, though, trying to find the right words to warn you . . .'

'Warn me——' a quiver of fear made her tremble. 'Milo,' she implored him anxiously, 'for goodness' sake, what about?'

He took a deep breath and stared unhappily at the floor. 'Guy left the hotel an hour ago looking like murder.'

'He did?' Alana went cold, but told herself she had no reason to feel unduly apprehensive. Guy's movements had nothing to do with her. Nor could she be held wholly responsible for the kind of mood he was in. She hadn't seen him since this morning, and when she had left him with Mrs Templeton he had been smiling.

When Milo merely nodded, without speaking, she asked unsteadily, 'Are you implying that I was the cause of Guy leaving the hotel in a rage?'

CHAPTER SEVEN

MILO's sighs became louder and he didn't quite meet her eyes. 'You've been seeing a lot of Fabian Marlow?'

What was Milo getting at? Alana frowned. 'Well, not seeing him exactly, not at least in the sense I think you mean. I've had a drink with him in the club and he's taken me out once to lunch. And once, when we bumped into each other outside, he bought me a coffee, but that's all.'

'Guy thinks you've been seeing a lot of each other.'

'Milo!' She was startled to hear her voice growing shrill and tried to control it. 'If you don't tell me what this is all about I'm going to scream!'

'You might scream when I do,' he prophesied darkly.

'I'll risk it,' she retorted tensely, eaten up by a mounting anxiety. 'Come on.'

But during the next few minutes, as she listened in frozen horror to his halting explanations, she wished she had never insisted.

'Guy had a phone call from Mr Marlow's future parents-in-law, or who were going to be Mr Marlow's future in-laws,' Milo began grimly. 'Apparently Mr Marlow had just been in touch with their daughter, Guy's second cousin incidentally, and cancelled their engagement. He told her he was in love with another girl—you. His fiancée, I believe, began screaming at her parents, threatening to take her own life, and before they could prevent her she rushed off in her car, which she proceeded to wreck, along with herself, against a stone wall. I don't know what Guy said to the girl's parents, he didn't say, but after he'd finished speaking to them he went to Mr Marlow's suite to tell him what had happened. Unfortunately he also found a letter from you to Fabian. Guy didn't divulge what was in it,' Milo assured Alana hastily, 'but it seems to have made him pretty mad.'

'Go on,' Alana whispered hoarsely, as Milo saw how white she had grown and paused. Once started, Milo had recounted what had happened, or what he had been told had happened, almost without pausing for breath, but she had been able to follow him and felt terribly shocked. Yet she had to know the rest. Was the girl still alive? 'Milo?' she entreated.

Milo did go on, but he appeared ill at ease, as if he wished he were somewhere else. 'I'm not enjoying this,' he muttered, running distracted fingers through his hair. 'From what I gathered Guy tackled Mr Marlow about your letter and Mr Marlow began shouting that he intended to marry you. But after Guy informed him of his fiancée's accident apparently he collapsed in a heap. It must have shocked him to his senses, because he asked Guy if he would take him to his fiancée immediately. He was still insisting he loved you, though, which made Guy suspicious. That's why he put Fabian in his car and then came to see me.'

'Why should he want to see you?' Alana asked hollowly.

'Guy and I have known each other since we were kids,' Milo answered evasively. 'He often tells me things. I'm afraid that after he's taken Fabian to the hospital in Hertfordshire, he's coming back here. Even if the girl is all right he intends suing you for the money you owe him and blackening your name so badly that no one else will ever employ you, nor will Fabian look at you again.'

Apprehensive tears filled Alana's eyes at this and she had some difficulty holding them at bay. She felt a terrible despair, not so much for her own safety as that

Guy should think so badly of her. Perhaps she deserved it, though. She must have been out of her mind to go to Fabian for money.

'Could Guy really do all that to me?' she asked, her voice shaking.

'I'm not sure, darling,' Milo replied heavily, 'but I'd be surprised if he didn't try. Have you ever seen him lose his temper?'

'I've seen him angry.'

'But not the ultimate?' Milo chewed his bottom lip, 'He's in a murderous mood, I can tell you. He's very fond of his cousin. I believe he was planning to give her an engagement party.'

'I had no intention of marrying Fabian,' Alana faltered. 'It was only——' Blushing unhappily, she broke off, reluctant to discuss all the details with Milo. He seemed to know too much already. 'What am I going to do?' she whispered to no one in particular.

'First you'd better drink this.' She hadn't been aware of Milo pouring her a drink. 'You look as if you need it,' he frowned. 'You've obviously had a shock.'

Alana almost choked. Hadn't Fabian said much the same thing only hours ago? A brief shudder ran through her as she took a small sip of the brandy to please Milo, then set it aside. She felt dreadful. The room momentarily swung around her and she was sure she was going to be sick. Even to think of Guy's anger was terrifying.

'Alana darling,' Milo propped himself against the side of the desk beside her, 'I don't know what's been going on, and I don't know that I want to know, either, but I can't believe you deserve the kind of punishment Guy has in mind. He asked me to keep you under close surveillance until he returns and will probably murder me if he ever finds out I offered to help, but I feel I can't just stand aside and let him crush you out of existence. Which,' he added darkly, 'for his cousin's sake, is what I'm sure he's going to try and do.'

Numbly Alana shook her head. The brandy should have warmed her a little, but she still felt icy cold. What was she to do? If only she could think of something! She would have to stay and face him, but it would be dreadful, for she had no real means of defending herself. Guy was clever, he might charge her with all sorts of things. She could even be in prison before her parents.

'How would you like to disappear for a few weeks?' to her amazement she heard Milo asking.

'Disappear?' She glanced at him, her eyes widening.

'That's what I said. Listen, darling,' he leaned forward, 'my eldest brother manages a hotel on the Italian island of Ischia. It's near Capri, in the Bay of Naples. His latest singer has just left him, or is about to leave him, I believe. They leave all the time,' he shrugged. 'As soon as the novelty of working in the Mediterranean wears off, they're gone. Well, by sheer coincidence, just after Guy left my brother rang, asking if I knew of a girl who'd be willing to fill in. Knowing what I did, I immediately thought this might be a way out for you? In fact, on the strength of it, I promised I'd almost certainly be sending someone. I even went so far as to ring the airport about a ticket. Nothing that can't be cancelled, of course,' he hastened to assure her.

A vague feeling of suspicion stirred at the back of Alana's mind. It was mixed with an uneasiness she didn't understand. 'Are you sure?' she asked doubtfully. 'I think I'm getting to be a bit wary of these sudden vacancies. You see, when I first came to London, Guy said there was a vacancy here . . .'

'And so there was,' Milo returned sharply, 'but a vacancy in a capital city, my pet, is much easier to fill than one on a remote island. Sure, we have girls who come and go, but this is no great problem. It just happened I wanted someone at the time and you're a nice little girl whom I took to immediately. Guy didn't deceive you about that! You suit me—and I know you'd suit Pascal just as well. And you'd be doing him a good turn if you stayed even a couple of weeks. I'd advise you to stay until Guy cools down and Fabian comes completely to his senses, but naturally that will be up to you.'

It was a big decision to make quickly, but this wasn't the main consideration, she supposed. In a daze, she stared at Milo. 'What would you tell Guy? Wouldn't he hold you responsible?'

'I'd say you ran away and I couldn't stop you.'

'Would he believe you?'

'He'd have to, wouldn't he?' Milo grunted. 'I'm not saying that would stop him trying to find you, but I doubt if he would think of looking for you on Ischia.'

Closing her eyes in an attempt to think more clearly, Alana failed. It made sense to run away and she could trust Milo. He wouldn't send her into any danger. He liked her, was even prepared to lie for her. Because she was so strung up, her eyes filled with nervous tears. 'I think I'll have to go,' she whispered eventually, trying to thank him. 'What else can I do?'

When he flushed and turned his head away, she thought she must be embarrassing him. 'I'll have to give my mother a ring first, though. Oh, I forgot,' she paused as he nodded, 'they aren't on the phone now. I'd better write.'

'Your parents are both alive?' As if he had antici-pated her needs, Milo pushed a pen and some paper towards her.

'Yes.' As usual she didn't want to talk about them for fear someone connected them with the money she had tried to borrow. Picking up the pen, she asked, 'Do I have to hurry?'

'I'm afraid so.'

Alana sat, her hand clenched tightly around the pen, despair in every line of her taut young body. All she could think of was the injured girl and Guy's fury. Yet it wasn't his anger she dreaded so much as his hate and contempt. And while she felt unable to stay and wait for him she despised herself for being a coward. But having read her note to Fabian, every begging, incriminating word of it, she could well imagine he would show her no mercy.

'When do I go?' she asked bleakly.

'Soon,' Milo replied briefly. 'I managed to get you a ticket and if your passport's in order you leave in just under two hours. I'll take you straight to the airport as soon as you've packed. Your fare will be paid and you will be met, so you don't have to worry about anything like that. You will be quite safe, I promise you. Just finish your letter and I'll post it while you throw a few things in a bag, then we'll be off.'

The island appeared to be very beautiful, but Alana was still too distraught to take in much detail. She had flown from Heathrow to Rome and from there to Naples, where she had stayed the night before flying on to Ischia. Here a car had met her and taken her to the hotel, a few miles along the coast from a place called Lacco Ameno.

The previous day she wanted only to forget. It must have been one of the worst in her life, beginning as it had done with her mother's letter and ending in what she could only think of as a full-scale disaster. When she had left England she had been too frightened and shocked to be able to judge if she was doing the right thing. Even now she still wasn't sure. She did know, though, that if Fabian's fiancée died she would never forgive herself and would hate herself for the rest of her life. She had made Milo promise he would ring her just as soon as he knew what the girl's condition was, and she found herself praying continually that the news would be good.

The Remma Hotel was situated on a beautiful stretch of beach. Alana caught a glimpse of it as they drove in to the rear of the hotel where the driver parked the car. She had also noticed two large swimming pools in the hotel grounds. Between the sea and the pools there must be plenty of choice if one wanted to swim!

The Remma was obviously in the luxury class. It was a huge, modern building, glistening white, offset by great splashes of colour supplied by the luxuriant vegetation. There were flowers and flowering shrubs everywhere, beautiful and exotic, and the warm, balmy air was fragrant with the scent of them. If she had come here on holiday, Alana knew she would have loved it, but she was very much aware that the price of such accommodation would, in normal circumstances, be way beyond her pocket.

She was taken to the manager by the driver, who seemed conscientious to a remarkable degree. Later it occurred to her that since first setting foot on Italian soil she had been looked after every minute. Milo had arranged for her to be taken to a hotel in Naples last night and someone had driven her to Naples Capodichino Airport this morning and waited until after she had flown off. It could only be her imagination that she had been kept under constant surveillance.

On the way to the manager's office, with her driver again in close attendance, she was conscious of people turning to glance at them. The guests, standing around in couples and small groups, probably imagined she was arriving royalty, coming in like this with a uniformed man who seemed to be guarding her every footstep.

To her surprise Milo's brother bore little physical resemblance to him. Facially she could find none, and being taller and thinner he had an elegance Milo lacked. His eyes were as kind as Milo's, though, which she found somehow reassuring.

Coming towards her as soon as she entered his office, he held out his hand with a warm smile. 'Good morning, Miss Hurst. I hope you had a good journey?'

Alana liked his firm handshake. 'It was rather a rush,' she admitted, 'but everything went quite smoothly.'

'Good,' he studied her closely, 'I'm glad to hear it.'

Beneath his close scrutiny she felt her cheeks grow hot and she wished she could lose the habit of blushing so easily. Because of her career she ought to have forgotten how to long ago. Pascal Sachs would merely be considering her potential, so why did she have this feeling that his scrutiny held more than a normal amount of interest?

'Milo said you wanted a singer urgently?' she queried as the silence became uncomfortable.

'Ah yes,' he replied quickly with another charming smile, 'and how is my disreputable brother?'

'Looking forward to seeing you in a few weeks' time,' she relayed Milo's message faithfully, 'and he's very well.'

'That is good to hear!' Pascal's rather austere face lit up, 'I see less of him than I would like to. Now I will get someone to take you to your room. Later you must meet my wife and daughter.'

'Thank you,' she said gravely, thinking how nice it would be to have some feminine company for a change. It wasn't until she was in her room and alone that she realised Milo's brother hadn't said a word about when she was to start work.

It must be, she decided anxiously, as she gazed nervously around the fourth room she had occupied in as many weeks, that he was giving her time to settle in. Broodingly she stared at her pale face and bruised eyes in the mirror. He probably thought she looked as though she needed a good rest before she was fit to do anything.

The room was nice, but she was learning not to place too much importance on things like nice accommodation which could be whisked away at a moment's notice. On opening a door at the far end of the room, she discovered it was a small bathroom, containing a basin and shower. She looked at the shower longingly, but decided to unpack first. The long dresses in her case must be hung up as soon as possible. There might be no immediate means of getting them pressed and, despite Pascal Sachs' silence on the matter, she didn't know how soon she might need them? Once they were safely hanging in the wall unit she surveyed what she had left with some dismay. In her haste to get away she appeared to have overlooked that she would need clothes for other occasions. She had brought only a couple of cotton skirts and tops apart from the jeans and shirt she was wearing.

Biting her lip, she hoped it wouldn't be long before her salary was paid. She had unfortunately sent all her surplus cash to her parents, before she left London, and apart from a few lire Milo had pressed into her hand she had nothing. She was virtually penniless.

Feeling she was growing unhealthily morbid, Alana did her best to cheer up, but it wasn't easy. The room was quiet, there was nothing to distract her unhappy thoughts. She didn't like to go out for fear Mr Sachs might send for her, but no one came near her for the rest of the morning. At one o'clock lunch was served in her apartment by a young Italian girl who could speak very little English.

When Alana smiled and said, '*Molto grazie,*' rather self consciously from the phrase book she had been studying, the girl merely smiled back. Trying again, she glanced at her lunch. '*Molto gentile,*' which, as far as she could make out was, 'It's very kind of you,' but the girl's smile merely widened and she shook her dark head.

When she had gone, Alana wondered belatedly if she would have had more success if she'd tried French, which she spoke fairly fluently. Perhaps she and the little maid could have talked to each other better in that language.

While her lunch was delicious, she still found herself unable to eat. She wished she could, as she hated wasting good food, but she suspected her appetite might not return until she learnt that Fabian's fiancée would live. Even then, with Guy's anger so much on her mind, she didn't think there would be much improvement. She wished she didn't love him so much, but she had never dreamt that falling in love would cause so much pain.

As she listlessly pushed *prosciutto di Parma con melone* around on her plate, she wondered if she would be expected to take all her meals in her room, or if she would be allowed to take them with the staff or in the dining-room with the guests. Today she appreciated the isolation, but she didn't know if she could stand it all the time. Getting up restlessly, she wandered to the window. She seemed to be high up on the side of the hotel. From her window she could see the sea, a wonderful blue, fairy-tale sea, and on her way here she had noticed the long crescents of sandy beaches and beautiful inlets. If only, she thought, suppressing a sob, she felt better and could get rid of a continual and frightening inclination to panic!

When the girl came to remove the remains of her meal, Alana asked if she could see the manager. The hours were slipping away and she was beginning to think everyone had forgotten about her. They couldn't believe she was all that much in need of a rest!

The manager had gone to Porto d'Ischia, the chief

town on the island. This much Alana was able to make out from the girl's halting English. It was not known when he would return.

Decidedly frustrated, when she was alone again, Alana almost resolved to go and discover for herself whether this was true or not. The girl probably wouldn't intentionally deceive her, but she could have made a mistake. Then she concluded that she might be wiser to take a shower and lie on her bed. She was tired, she felt too tense to sleep, but if she lay down it might make her feel better. And it would pass the time, if nothing else.

Hours later she was awakened by someone knocking on her door. Because the knocking sounded urgent she didn't wait to dress but hurried to open it still in her thin robe. Realising just how thin it was, she was relieved to find her caller was only the girl who had been looking after her.

'Yes?' she prompted, as the girl stared at her, as though she had never seen such a mass of golden hair before.

Alana gathered that she was to go to suite 100 and the girl would wait to take her there. After asking the maid to come in and wait, she rinsed her face again and put on one of her cotton skirts. Swiftly she smoothed a little make-up over her face to hide its pallor and brushed out her hair. Slipping her feet into sandals, she thought she might do. If it was the manager who wanted to see her she didn't want to keep him waiting.

Following the maid, she was again struck by the sheer luxury of the hotel and hoped bleakly it would bring her more luck than the Remax. She was anxious that there was as yet no word from Milo and resolved to mention to his brother that she was expecting a call from him. In a hotel this size it might be very easy for a message to go astray.

The girl took her to what was obviously a private wing, right at the top of the hotel. On Alana's floor it had been quiet, but here there was no noise at all. Her escort paused by a door and rang the bell, then, to Alana's surprise, walked away. She was still gazing after her, unsure what to make of it, when the door opened. At first she didn't hear it, it was only when she became conscious of an odd but terribly familiar prickling down her spine that she swung around with a gasp. Guy Renwick was standing in the doorway staring at her, his eyes colder than she could ever remember seeing them.

'Oh, no!' she gasped, her voice seeming as disembodied as her senses, as with a smothered moan she found everything going black. She tried to save herself, but the last thing she was conscious of was of someone catching her, picking her up and holding her close.

When she came around she found she was lying on a couch and Guy was wetting her lips with brandy. He had his arm behind her head, supporting her, but although he wasn't hurting her his whole stance was far from gentle.

'Don't pass out on me again,' he snapped as her eyes opened. 'Next time I won't believe it!'

Blankly she stared at him, feebly pushing away the brandy. She was getting tired of men thrusting brandy at her. First Fabian, then Milo, now Guy, and all of them determined to deceive rather than help her. Milo's deception must be the worst of the lot, as he must have told Guy where she was.

'I never thought Milo would do it,' she said bitterly, 'I really believed he was my friend.'

'He was only obeying orders.'

'Orders?' she whispered, the shock of learning this shaking her so much she feared she might be going mad. 'You mean you told him to send me here?'

'It was easier than kidnapping, and more dignified

for you,' he retorted, withdrawing his arm and rising swiftly to his feet. From where he was standing his eyes went slowly and insolently over her, but she could read nothing else from his expression. There was only ice in the grey depths.

Feeling she might fight him better from a less recumbent position, she sat up. Her pulse had stopped racing, but it was still far from steady. Defiantly she met his arrogant gaze. 'You might have tricked me into coming here, but I won't stay, and you can't make me. I'll see the manager. If he is the manager—or Milo's brother?' she breathed, a frightening suspicion suddenly gripping her.

'He's both,' Guy reassured her coolly, 'but he also happens to be my employee.' As she gasped incredulously, he went on, without noticeable compunction, 'I own this hotel, it belongs to my company. So you see, my dear, you won't be able to rely on any help from Pascal.'

Alana jumped to her feet, anger supplementing the strength which two days without food had depleted. 'I'd like to murder you!' she cried tempestuously.

His mouth curled derisively, 'Wasn't Fabian's fiancée enough?'

'Oh,' Alana swayed, her face going so pale his eyes narrowed in satisfaction. 'How is she? She—she isn't any worse?'

'No thanks to you, she isn't,' he rapped. 'I believe she'll recover eventually.'

His words hurt and she flinched but said steadily, 'I'm glad. I was very sorry to hear of her accident.'

'Always full of regret after the deed is done, aren't you?' he sneered.

'It wasn't intentional. I can explain.' Desperately she added, as his eyes glittered with contempt, 'If Milo hadn't frightened me away I would have stayed and explained to you in London.'

Suddenly Guy was furious. 'Don't try pleading innocence with me, Miss Hurst. It won't wash any more. You took me for a fool the first time you saw me and maybe you were right, because I certainly should have summed you up better than I did. If I'd had any sense at all I'd have ran a mile. You weren't looking for a job, you were after a sucker to bleed for his cash. First you took me for five hundred, then Fabian for double the amount. What you'd planned for the next poor fool I shudder to think! It must be up to me to teach you a lesson you won't ever forget, for the sake of my fellow men if nothing else!'

'You're wrong!' She was white to the lips at his harsh castigation. 'I only asked for a loan. I was busy repaying you and I would have repaid Fabian every penny too.'

'I'd rather not waste time discussing it,' he dismissed what she said with obvious contempt. 'If it had only concerned me I would have left you in London to face the consequences, but I wasn't going to let you stay anywhere near Fabian. He and my cousin were happy enough before you came on the scene and they'll be happy again. If you want a millionaire you'll have to look farther afield.'

'I don't want to marry Fabian,' she cried wildly, pleading with him although she knew she had already lost. 'Can't you believe me?'

'Never in a thousand years,' he exclaimed savagely. 'And if you think I should have more compassion, how much did you have for my cousin? You were aware of Fabian's forthcoming marriage, because he told you, yet you let him break off his engagement without a word of protest. Even if you'd been in love with him, which I don't believe you are, there is such a thing as honour.'

'It wasn't like that,' she protested, dismay reducing her voice to a mere whisper. But how could she convince him without condemning her parents?

'How was it, then?' Guy jeered, his eyes like flint.

Alana concentrated on Fabian. 'I realise I should have made myself plainer, but I—I had something else on my mind.'

'Which is unexplainable, apparently?' he taunted silkily, as she paused, distracted.

Numbly she nodded, overwhelmed by despair.

'Speechless, are you?' he laughed. 'Well, you'll be more than speechless before I'm through with you. You might just wish you hadn't been born, Miss Hurst. And if you do escape without any permanent evidence of your folly, I'll make sure no decent man will ever want to know you again!'

It was too much. Whatever she had done, Alana didn't think she deserved to be spoken to like this. 'You're despicable!' she cried, her hand shooting out to contact his hard face.

The jerk which lifted her against him almost robbed her of her senses again, and the pain as he gripped a handful of her long, fair hair made her wince. Then his mouth descended, curved in cruel lines of fury, to crush hers brutally, while the hand he used to hold her to him dug deep into her helpless flesh.

It was only as her knees buckled that he released her, his breathing as erratic as her own. As the fire within her died down she knew another urge to hit out at him, but a breath of caution warned her it could be dangerous to arouse his anger any further. Brokenly she stared at him, knowing she hated him, believing this might be the one good thing to come out of the assault he had made on her.

Controlling her bruised lips with difficulty, she managed to speak reasonably clearly. 'You must see how impossible it would be for us to have anything more to do with each other?' A flicker of hope prompted her to add, 'If I promised not to go back to

London, Guy, would you be prepared to let me go?'

'No,' the eyes coolly watching her flushed face didn't soften a fraction, 'I don't trust you an inch.'

'But you can't keep me prisoner!'

'Not in chains,' his brows rose indifferently, 'but if you attempt to run away you'll regret it. I could have you arrested for fraud. You're a singer who was beginning to be known, and the newspapers would be only too keen to make a story out of it.'

'You can't be serious?' she gasped, but had no means of discovering whether he was or not.

'Try it and see,' he suggested smoothly.

While she digested this in unhappy silence, his eyes narrowed. When she said nothing more about leaving, he asked coldly, 'This money you were trying to borrow from Fabian, what did you want it for?'

'Nothing much,' she murmured indistinctly.

He refused to be put off. 'A thousand pounds is a lot of money, even today. You must have had some idea?'

'Clothes, perhaps,' she replied vaguely, 'but I didn't get anything, so what does it matter?'

'The truth matters,' he said tersely, 'and I'll get it out of you, even if it takes months!'

Months? Anxiously her eyes widened. Guy had tricked her here. Milo's brother didn't require a singer. He had been embarrassed when she had mentioned it; she remembered the look on his face even if she hadn't understood it at the time. She needed some money, though, so it was imperative she began earning. 'I'll have to find some work,' she said.

'You can assist me,' he snapped, 'I was coming to that. After all, you still have to repay what you owe me, and you won't be doing any more singing.'

Alana had to accept this for the moment, but she gazed at him incredulously. 'What could I do to help you?' she asked. 'I'm not trained as a secretary.'

'I don't need a secretary,' he retorted, 'or when I

do I borrow Pascal's, but I do need a personal assistant.
And when I don't need you,' he added, 'you can stay
in your room or make yourself as invisible as possible.
If I see you talking to anyone in the hotel I can think
of a much less agreeable prison. I own an island where
I occasionally go when I feel like my own company.
Believe me, it's so basic and rough you wouldn't enjoy
it in the least.'

What made him think she wouldn't? It sounded like
paradise to what she might have to put up with here.
'You might have some explaining to do if I haven't to
talk to anyone,' she muttered, daring a single note of
defiance. 'Mr Sachs said he would like me to meet his
wife and daughter.'

'I'll consider it,' Guy said curtly, promising
nothing.

Alana's hands curled into tight fists as she contemplated long hours spent alone with her unhappy
thoughts. Why did she have the feeling that none of
this could really be happening to her? It was hard to
believe, yet so were a lot of other things. Wasn't it as
difficult to associate the grim-eyed stranger confront-
ing her with the man who had once been so kind?

'What about my meals?' she asked, then wondered
why she had mentioned them when she never felt
hungry.

Ignoring the tears in her eyes, he replied shortly,
'You'll take them in your room, all but dinner. That
you can eat in one of the dining-rooms. I'll arrange for
a table to be reserved for you. Where I can see what
you're doing!'

No invitation to dine with him, she noticed. 'Thank
you,' she whispered, striving to control herself, her
heart sinking as her humble words of appreciation
received only a harsh glance. 'What exactly are my
duties to be?' she enquired, as the silence lengthened
and he made no effort to break it.

Tauntingly, he smiled. 'Running errands, taking notes, generally keeping me happy. The social side of life here can get a bit complicated. You'll have to see that mine runs smoothly. I don't want to find I've arranged to take two women out to dinner on the same night, or made arrangements to attend an event when I already have another engagement.'

'I see.' She lowered her heavy lashes for fear he should read the anguish in her eyes. She wasn't sure whether she was meant to take all he said seriously, but it hurt. How could they work together with so much bitterness between them? she wondered desperately.

When he muttered sharply, 'You can start at nine in the morning,' she nodded bleakly and left him.

After managing to get through the door with her head held high, in her room she broke down and sobbed, shedding the tears she had found so difficult to restrain before. She could scarcely believe what had happened. The shock of it was just beginning to really hit her. It had been a shattering experience to be confronted unexpectedly by a man whom one had never expected to see again. And, apart from Guy, there was Milo! It wounded her deeply that he had been willing to deceive her, although, looking back, she suspected he hadn't found it easy. He had been on edge all the time, and unable to meet her eyes.

But if he had deceived her without difficulty, how could she blame him? The evidence against her was pretty conclusive and Guy would have been convincing. Had she not been so gullible she might have realised something was very wrong, for she recalled being slightly suspicious. No, she could scarcely condemn either Guy or Milo when they must both have believed they were acting for the best. And, even if her parents sold the house, there was no way she could compensate for the suffering she had inadvertently caused Fabian's fiancée. Perhaps, Alana decided, with a sigh, to stay here, out of the way might, as Guy said, be the best way of putting things right.

CHAPTER EIGHT

THE next few days proved nerve-racking ones for Alana. She began working for Guy and he let it be known she was there as his personal assistant. That this attracted some speculative glances was bad enough, but Alana found it even more humiliating when she discovered he had told Pascal she had a secret ambition to become a singer but when he had given her a chance at the Remax she hadn't been a success.

'She is more fitted for what she is doing,' he said smoothly, when Pascal mentioned the subject somewhat apologetically, the first day before lunch on inviting them to have a drink in his office.

Pascal agreed. 'She has too much reticence in her eyes to make a success of that kind of career. I saw it immediately,' his kind smile took any sting from his words. 'For cabaret a girl needs more than the usual amount of confidence.'

'Exactly.' Guy hid his cynicism cleverly. Only Alana appeared to notice it as his eyes studied her with familiar insolence.

Wishing desperately that she could be immune to his undoubted good looks, she glanced away from him. She could feel her blood tingling with a new and disturbing sensation that made her shiver. She wanted to strike back at him because of it, but couldn't.

She didn't dare speak up for herself, not even when Pascal, noting her tenseness and mistaking it for confusion, said laughing, 'Never mind, Miss Hurst, people might regard you more kindly for following a more conventional career. Our glamorous singers are much admired, but perhaps for this very reason often have to put up with a deal deal of distrust and suspicion.'

Despite Pascal's ponderous and rather obvious attempts to pour oil on troubled waters, Alana felt sure he meant well and smiled at him. She tried to ignore Guy's secret, derisive amusement. 'I'm sure they don't always deserve such censure,' she remarked.

'No,' Pascal agreed soberly. 'Most of them are ordinary, decent girls like yourself, only trying to earn an honest living.'

'If that were all,' Guy drawled thinly.

Alana flushed at his blatant insinuation, which she understood if Pascal didn't. Was he never to miss a opportunity of reminding her of her sins?

Pascal's phone rang and after answering it he said, 'My wife and daughter are eager to meet you, Miss Hurst. I wondered if we might all dine together this evening, Guy?'

'By all means,' Guy nodded blandly, 'I'd be delighted, but I don't know about Miss Hurst. I believe she prefers to dine alone. An odd idiosyncrasy, I admit, but one I allow her.'

Because she felt so indignant, Alana forgot their agreement and found the courage to defy him. How dared he attempt to make her turn down such an innocent invitation? Lifting her fair head, she smiled at Pascal warmly. 'I'm afraid Mr Renwick gets some strange ideas. I would love to meet your wife and daughter, Mrs Sachs. I'd be delighted to share a meal with you.'

She managed to avoid Guy for the rest of the afternoon, and surprisingly he didn't send for her. A severe reprimand was the least she had expected after defying him so openly, and escaping it in Pascal's office was no guarantee he wouldn't pounce once they were alone.

When he went out for a few hours, leaving her to her own devices, she didn't know what to think. Any relief soon disappeared beneath the uneasy conviction that he had some far more subtle revenge planned for later on.

As she began getting ready for dinner, she suddenly realised she would have to wear one of her night club dresses as she had nothing else. Despairingly she tried them all on, finally choosing the more modest of the five. Even this was too revealing for her liking, and she stared at her reflection with a frown. Her fair hair swung like a heavy silk curtain and, as she hadn't had time to acquire a tan, her skin was milk-white. Her mouth, which she coudn't remember noticing before, didn't please her much either; it seemed a shade too full beneath her small, delicate nose. But there was nothing, she insisted to herself, to suggest the immodesty Guy was always hinting at. If it hadn't been for her dress, which unfortunately showed rather too much of her gently curved figure, she was certain she looked more decorous than the majority of her generation. And she could never recall using her physical attractions to get her own way.

She found Guy talking to the group of people with whom apparently they were to dine. He had sent someone to escort her from her room, and while she was relieved he hadn't come himself, she wondered why he had deprived himself of the pleasure of dragging her along. As he noted her dress, she saw him mouth thin, and was aware of his contemptuous disapproval. He would just have to disapprove, she met his eyes defiantly, for she wasn't going to begin explaining before his sophisticated friends how she had forgotten to bring one of her own dresses.

Pascal was there with a small, dark woman whom he introduced as his wife. His daughter, Paula, was dark, too, and very pretty and friendly. Alana liked Pascal's

family immediately and they chatted until it was time
to go in to dinner. Guy, apart from a frequent harsh
glance, didn't speak to her.

He appeared to have attached himself to a tall, wil-
lowy creature, who reminded Alana vaguely of Mrs
Templeton. During dinner, which began to seem
never-ending, Alana noticed he gave her most of his
attention. Paula whispered that she was called Ellis
Lane and had been married three times, and she
believed Guy had known her a long time. When Alana
asked where the current husband was, Paula remarked
mischievously that there wasn't one at the moment,
but Miss Lane was said to be looking for her fourth.

Guy must have a weakness for widows and divor-
cees. Watching him from under her heavy lashes, Alana
wondered why the sight of him being so charming to
another woman could still make her feel so sick.
Catching his glance, she looked away again quickly,
but not before she caught a glimpse of the cold mockery in his eyes.

Apart from the manager and his family and Miss
Lane, there were four other people at their table, all
apparently old friends of Guy's, but Alana felt no
special interest in any one of them. Nor did she find it
easy to pretend to, not even when the youngest man,
the son of the elderly couple sitting opposite, tried to
engage her in conversation. He was pleasant and obviously attracted, but the gold watch he wore and the
quality of his clothes screamed of wealth. She was so
afraid Guy might accuse her of trying to obtain money
from him that she scarcely dared utter a word. Ron
Adamson might dismiss her from his thoughts as a
dumb blonde, but it couldn't be helped.

After dinner, when Guy suggested they should all
go down to the cellar discotheque, she wanted badly to
refuse. There would be a singer, she suspected, and it
might be Guy's cruel intention to show her what she

was missing, but she couldn't find the strength to fight him. The events of the day were fast catching up on her and she felt curiously indifferent.

The cellar, purpose-built, might, in fact, be quite entitled to the name, but it was vastly different from any cellar Alana had ever known. It was below ground, but there any comparison ended. The lights were dimmed and it was a huge room with the usual tables set round the perimeter of the dance floor. Every table was taken, but naturally one was soon found for the owner and his guests. Alana hoped her bitterness didn't show as she sat down. The cabaret was good, she could see they certainly weren't short of acts, which increased her sense of disillusionment as she realised again how easily she had been fooled.

She was just trying to think of a way of slipping out unnoticed when to her surprise Guy asked her to dance. 'Don't waste your breath refusing,' he said coolly, swinging her away in his arms.

She had danced with him once before and still remembered too clearly to risk a repeat. Yet what could she do? As she turned her head to meet the challenging gleam in his grey eyes, her heart began to pound. Their gaze held and her breath shortened, but she managed to gasp, 'I don't know why you should want to dance with me, seeing how your opinion of me is so low.'

'Wouldn't people think it rather strange if I didn't dance at least once with my personal assistant?' he drawled.

In whichever fields he had achieved success, mockery must be one of them! Angrily, Alana wrenched her hypnotised eyes from his. 'I don't think anyone would notice. I can't imagine the kind of people you have here would bother their beautiful heads about such things.'

'Your own head isn't all that bad,' he drawled. 'It's what's inside it . . .'

Well, she had asked for that one, hadn't she? She wanted to insult him back, but couldn't seem to make the effort. 'May I go to my room after this?' she pleaded, her blue eyes huge with strain as she glanced up at him again.

Guy drew her closer, as though to shut out the sight, holding her so tightly her head was forced against his shoulder. A wave of pleasure went down her spine as his warm hand pressed on the bare skin exposed by the low back of her dress.

He murmured something against the top of her head which she didn't catch, but might have been his consent to her query. She couldn't be sure and didn't want to ask as they circled the dance floor in silence, losing themselves in the seductive beat of the music. The floor was crowded, but there was still room to move and Guy demonstrated his not inconsiderable skill. His movements were intricate, but Alana, light on her feet, was no novice herself and followed him with ease.

Pulling her even tighter into his embrace, he gave a quick turn, his cheek resting intimately against her face. And again, as he had done before, his hand moved sensuously down her back, forcing her hips tightly against his. Pausing on a drumbeat, he swung her swiftly around, inserting one leg between her own, and at the pressure of the full length of his body she gasped and tried to pull back.

His hold only tightened and there was nothing she could do, short of creating a scene. She was conscious of curious glances without actually seeing them, while her love for him threatened to overwhelm her because of the blatant stimulation it was receiving. There was hate in her heart, too, for the publicity which he appeared to have no qualms about attracting.

'Please!' she quivered, at the mocking triumph in his eyes, her pride forgotten as her traitorous thighs responded shamelessly to the pressure he was exerting and her stomach muscles began contracting in a way she didn't understand. 'Please let me go, Guy.'

'Are you going to beg?' he asked softly in her ear, sensing the tension behind her plea. His warm breath sent feathery shivers around her nape, forcing her to breathe deeply in order to retain her sanity.

'If you like.' She made herself speak lightly, terrified that he might guess how she was tottering on the brink of abject surrender. 'Is this one of your methods of exacting revenge?' she asked.

As his hands tightened until she could have cried out with pain, she realised her choice of words had been unfortunate. 'You get brighter by the minute,' he jeered softly, 'how did you guess?'

'It wasn't very difficult,' she replied tautly, 'but surely enough is enough? Can I go to my room!'

'Not yet,' he snapped, suddenly releasing her, as if the game he had been playing no longer amused him. 'I'm taking two or three of my guests up to my suite, the married couple you were talking to and Miss Lane. I want you to come and pour the drinks and look after them for me.'

'You mean,' Alana raised anxious blue eyes to his, 'as your hostess?'

'No,' he retorted coldly, 'as my servant.'

This seemed to set the pattern for the week that followed. Guy used and treated her exactly like a servant. It might not have been apparent to anyone else, most of the other staff seemed to think she was actually a secretary and simply consented to these other duties when she hadn't much else to do. Oddly, Guy appeared to encourage this impression, for occasionally he asked her to type something on the machine he had in a room he used as his office, next door to his suite. If her somewhat laborious efforts took time, he didn't object, or appeared too dissatisfied with the results. Sometimes Alana suspected it was the concentrated

effort on her part which it took to produce anything
half decent which gave him such sadistic pleasure. It
also seemed to please him that she was growing thinner
and paler, and the more haunted she looked, the harder
he made her work.

It was amazing, she thought one evening, as she sat
at her solitary table eating her dinner, just how much
Guy found for her to do in an establishment so flooded
with staff. All day, from nine in the morning until late
at night, she fetched and carried and ran errands—a
lot of which, she considered privately, could have been
done much quicker by telephone. He even loaned her
to his friend Miss Lane, to help with her shopping,
and as Miss Lane's plans for the future obviously
included Guy, Alana had spent a far from enjoyable
afternoon.

Guy was dining with Miss Lane tonight. They sat at
a table not far from hers, so she was unable to avoid
looking at them occasionally. Hoping to avoid this, she
had asked him, with deliberate carelessness, what time
he was dining. He had shot her a quick glance and
replied just as carelessly—but now, she suspected, mis-
leadingly—that he had arranged to eat with Miss Lane
at nine-thirty. As it was only eight, he must have lied
about the time.

Why? Pondering the question, Alana felt close to
tears. She didn't want to see Guy at all, but her eyes
had a curious habit of straying in his direction. Was
this why he had chosen that particular table? So she
could see what a striking couple Miss Lane and he
made? He so tall and handsome and Miss Lane
smoothly lovely, like a well fed reptile.

Unable to believe the bitchy trend of her thoughts,
Alana flushed and caught Guy staring at her. At the
dislike in her eyes, which had been aimed at his companion, his mouth hardened and his glance became
threatening.

'I'll deal with you later, my girl,' he conveyed, as surely as if he had spoken.

Ron Adamson had asked her to have a drink with him after dinner, but she went to her room instead. She felt in no mood to exchange small talk with a boy of her own age, yet she was impatient with herself because of it. Ron and she were both nineteen, they might have had fun together and it needn't have been serious. And, if she was clever, Guy needn't have known about it. He was with Ellis Lane and he couldn't keep an eye on her all the time.

The two previous evenings after dinner, when she had ventured on to the terrace for a breath of fresh air, he had sought her out and accused her of attempting to mingle with the guests. This she hadn't been doing. All she had had in mind was a short walk in the star-studded night, but she hadn't even tried to explain. She was learning the hard way that any attempt to vindicate herself met with instant failure. Guy was so determined, it seemed, to think the worst of her that such an exercise was a sheer waste of breath.

Yet didn't she deserve his censure, if only because of Fabian's fiancée? Niggling doubts kept her awake when she went early to bed, and at last, quite sure she wasn't going to get to sleep, she got up. During the next few minutes she realised she would have to escape from her room, for at least a short while. She found it suffocating to the point where she could bear it no longer. She would liked to have gone for a swim, but she had no swimsuit or money to buy one. Then, in the act of reaching for her jeans, she paused. That afternoon, Ellis Lane and Guy had been swimming in one of the pools, and Guy had taken Alana along. It puzzled her that he frequently ordered her to accompany him when he took Miss Lane out and she often wondered what Miss Lane thought of it. Ellis didn't think much, Alana could tell, and unfortunately she

chose to vent her spite on Alana. That afternoon, after
the swimming session was over, she had given Alana
her wet bikini and told her to see it was washed and
pressed and returned to her room.

Alana viewed it eagerly. She had been angry that
Miss Lane obviously believed she had the right to treat
her as a servant. It was enough that Guy did. But she
remembered bleakly how he had stood, his powerful
body bare, apart from a pair of brief trunks, his glittering gaze trained on her, his rapier tongue, ready, she
sensed, to annihilate her on the spot, should she dare
to object. So she had accepted the bikini meekly, instead of throwing it back in Miss Lane's charming face.
She had even managed to stay silent when the taunting
expression in Guy's eyes congratulated her on being
sensible.

At this moment, feeling wearily near to breaking
point, Alana was indifferent to his disapproval. He
could be vexed or pleased—well, he certainly wouldn't
be the latter, but she was going for a swim. The yellow
bikini proved an irresistible temptation. She had
thought of trying to borrow a suit from Paula Sachs,
but Paula had gone to Milan to visit relatives and it
was not known when she would be home again.

The bra top of the bikini was tight and the bottom
too slack, but after a little careful adjustment she
decided it would do. But catching a glimpse of herself
in the mirror, before covering it with a shirt and jeans,
she blushed. Like the gowns she was forced to wear
night after night for dinner, it left little to the imagination. She was thankful that as it was after midnight no
one was likely to see her.

On the odd occasion when she had managed to leave
the hotel undetected, she had noticed if any of the
guests swam after dark it was in one of the pools near
the building itself. The third, some distance away, was
usually deserted. It was rather lonely and surrounded

by trees, and if people were inclined to wander in the moonlight they appeared to favour the beach or some well lit corner of the grounds.

The dressing cabins, with their showers and ample changing rooms, were locked, and Alana got the fright of her life when, scrambling out of her clothes where she stood, she was almost drowned by a shower of water.

'Got you!' a male voice cried.

It was Ron Adamson. She nearly fainted with relief and felt like laughing, but she couldn't let him off so lightly. 'Are you crazy?' she exclaimed, hiding a grin. 'I might have had a heart attack!'

'You're too young,' he laughed from the side of the pool. 'Kids of our age don't have such things.'

'How do you know?' she began laughing, too. 'Anyway, it's not funny.'

'You're doing most of the laughing, love,' he teased.

'Which doesn't prove anything,' she retaliated, finding a certain relaxation in such lighthearted, inconsequential banter.

'It proves you need my company,' he replied, a fraction more soberly. 'I wasn't sure you knew how to laugh.'

Despite this shrewd remark, Alana was surprised to find she felt happier than she had done since she came. It proved she should mix more. But how could she, with Guy breathing fire and brimstone down her neck all the time, threatening dreadful things?

Perhaps she should try to persuade him to give her more freedom? Today he had heard that Fabian's fiancée was out of hospital and almost well once more. When Alana had asked about the engagement, he had glanced at her sharply but said it was still on, and he had every intention of seeing it wasn't broken again. The suspicion had still been there, but somehow, because the girl had recovered, Alana didn't feel quite so bad about it.

Now, deciding she could forget her prevailing sense of responsibility, if only for a little while, she asked Ron how long he had been swimming.

'About an hour,' he replied with a whimsical grin. 'I have a beach-ball,' he added, tempting her, 'but it's not much fun on my own.'

'A beach-ball?' she gazed at it, as he produced it, dubiously. 'It's after midnight!'

'So what?' he teased. 'You sound like an old woman!'

Who could resist such a challenge? 'Come on, then,' she giggled, diving into the pool, determined to prove she was not. The water was still warm, and she knew a wonderful sense of freedom as she swam through it neatly, and for the next half hour Ron and she played like a couple of young porpoises.

They were climbing out, Ron declaring he had had enough and was going back to the hotel and bed, when they both became aware of someone watching them. It didn't take Alana more than two seconds to recognise the tall figure standing stiffly at the end of the pool. It was Guy Renwick!

As fright ran through her, she brushed her long wet hair from her eyes, determined to brazen it out. 'Why, hello!' she called. 'Did you think the prisoner had escaped?'

Her tone, which she didn't realise was so insolent, appeared to jar him, but he didn't reply. His eyes glittered but that was all.

Ron said politely, for this man was a tycoon of some prominence and a friend of his father's, 'I'm sorry, sir, I didn't see you. Alana and I were too busy enjoying ourselves.'

'Enjoying yourselves?' Guy automatically grasped Alana by the arm, to help her from the pool, and both his grip and his voice stung.

'We were playing,' Ron said awkwardly.

Alana frowned, conscious that Guy still held her. Did Ron really feel it necessary to explain what they had been doing? He had lost the ball, having thrown it so high it had sailed away over the tops of the nearby trees. This was the real reason they had decided to call it a day, but, without the ball, she could almost guess the kind of interpretation Guy was placing on the scene.

'Do you realise the time?' he was asking Ron coldly.

'Just about one. Not late at our age,' the boy grinned. 'We were just on our way in, though. Coming, Alana?'

'I'll bring Miss Hurst back.' Guy was tight-lipped with anger.

'You're sure?' Ron glanced uncertainly from him to Alana.

Before she could intervene, Guy said curtly, 'I'm Miss Hurst's employer. I have something I wish to discuss, and I'm quite capable of looking after her.'

Ron acknowledged defeat with a brief lift of his hand and disappeared.

As he left, Alana rounded on Guy angrily. 'You needn't have been so abrupt with him. He's a nice boy and he wasn't committing any crime.'

'I didn't accuse him of any,' Guy retorted. 'You were the one at fault, by being out here.'

'I wasn't trying to run away!' she emphasised each word between closed teeth.

'But probably trying to persuade someone to help you to do so tomorrow? Don't tell me you wouldn't like to go?'

'Of course I'd like to go!' She didn't say because she was finding the situation intolerable, loving him as she did. He would simply laugh at her. When he didn't reply, she glanced at him again. 'You told Ron you had something to discuss. What was it?'

'Nothing that can't wait,' he shrugged, his eyes going

narrowly over her. 'That bikini looks familiar.'

Alana could feel her cheeks growing hot in the darkness, but decided to be honest. 'It belongs to Miss Lane, I borrowed it.'

'Without mentioning it to her?'

'I'm not a fool.'

'Did you think it's smarter than your own?'

Alana didn't know where this conversation was supposed to be getting them, but she felt she had to put an end to it. She couldn't stand here any longer with Guy's eyes dissecting every inch of her anatomy. 'If you must know,' she burst out impulsively, 'I haven't any. At least, the only one I have is at home in Manchester, and I haven't any money to buy another.'

'No money?' His brows rose hatefully.

'Until you pay me.'

'You certainly did leave London in a hurry,' he drawled, mockingly, 'forgetting the most important thing in your life.'

Without bothering to contradict him, she said tersely, 'Now that you know, may I go in? I think I need a hot shower.'

'You'd better have one here,' he advised curtly. 'If you imagine you're going to give the night porters a treat you're mistaken.'

'I have my jeans,' she could see them lying behind him in a heap, 'I'll put them on.'

'How can you?' He had released her wrist but as she made to go round him, he grabbed her again. 'You're dripping wet, I can feel.'

'The cabins are locked,' she suddenly recalled, in desperation, puzzled as to why she should feel so apprehensive.

'I have a key,' he explained smoothly, while his hands squeezed a dribble of water from her hair. 'Sometimes, at this time of night when it's quiet, I come for a swim. The pool's handy, but I prefer the sea.'

'Don't let me stop you,' she snapped. 'If you open a changing room door I can manage.'

'I've changed my mind about a swim,' he rejoined coolly. 'I'll wait for you.'

What could she do? Helplessly Alana looked down on her damp limbs. At a pinch she could get into her jeans, but it would be uncomfortable.

'Oh, very well!' she muttered, not very graciously.

Guy found the key, but the lock was stiff and he had some difficulty in turning it. As he struggled with it, the fact that the lock needed attention obviously aroused his impatience. This he vented on Alana. 'Just what the hell were you and young Adamson playing at?'

'We did have a ball!' she snapped back. 'It's somewhere in those trees.'

'I wasn't born yesterday!'

'No one's arguing about that,' she jeered unwisely. As his eyes darkened with quick fury, she jerked from him defensively. 'Whatever we were doing, is it any of your business? At the worst, it would be a lot more innocent than the things you and Miss Lane get up to!'

It must have been a mistake to go on provoking him. As the door gave way, he suddenly reached for her, lifting her off her feet and clear through it. Still holding her against him, he kicked it savagely shut behind him.

'Now, Miss Insolence,' he muttered, 'let's see just how good at games you are!'

Guy was dressed but had discarded his white dinner jacket and tie in favour of casual pants and a body shirt, obviously with the intention of going swimming. Now, as he held her close, striding his way towards one of the benches without putting on a light, she could feel every vital movement of his hard, muscled body.

Panic-stricken, she begged wildly, 'I'm sorry, Guy. Please let me go.'

'Not yet. I think I've earned a few moments of your time. You're very generous with others.'

Alana felt herself grow rigid. 'If I am,' she hissed, 'how about you and other women? You parade them endlessly and expect me . . .'

'Yes?' he prompted silkily, as she paused. 'I expect what?'

It came out in a panting rush, and indiscreetly, 'You expect me to behave like a nun until you want me.'

'Ha!' She could see his teeth gleaming white through the darkness, feel his breath on her face as he threw her down on one of the long benches and flung himself on top of her. 'I'm glad you get the message, Miss Hurst. You're wrong about the other women, but not about my wanting you.'

His weight, and the way her heart was hammering, made her dizzy. Without adding anything more to his unequivocal statement, he slowly lowered his head and began kissing her. At first his mouth was seductive and lazy, soothing the tumultuous thoughts in her head and the apprehensive tension from her limbs. The cabin was warm and, drugged by the gentleness of his kisses, she felt all desire to struggle leave her. Unconsciously one of her arms encircled his neck while the other rounded his waist, gripping tightly.

Guy responded instantly by tightening his own hold and forcing her lips farther apart, this and the increasing weight of his body bringing both pain and pleasure. His caresses became rougher and more demanding, but she made no more requests to be allowed to go. Her own response was beginning to frighten her, but there seemed nothing she could do about it. Recklessly she pressed him closer. His hair felt thick and silky to her fingers, and tentatively she slid an exploratory hand under his shirt.

He almost removed what was left of her ragged breath when with a swift movement he threw it off. And she gasped as he expertly reversed their positions, so she was lying on top of him. Then, with the same quickness with which he had got rid of his shirt, he unhooked her bikini and flung it aside, so there was not even the barrier of thin cloth between them.

'Guy!' she choked, the last remnants of her modesty raising an outcry as she slumped helplessly against him.

'Don't talk,' he commanded thickly.

'I . . .' she tried to find her voice, but it just wasn't there any more. It seemed to have degenerated into broken whimpers, with her breath catching in her throat in shuddering gulps.

His hand followed her waist, moving to the throbbing softness of her breasts, then held her still while he lifted her to ravage her pink peaks with his tongue and teeth. She felt his mouth, insistent and searching until she thought she would go out of her head with excitement and pleasure. Violent, uncontrollable desire rushed through her as he pressed her passionately against the whole length of his body.

Swiftly, his breathing heavy and erratic, he changed places with her again and the intimacy of their embrace was strengthened. He returned to her mouth, recapturing it with rough, burning kisses, which threatened to destroy the last of her senses. All his movements were becoming deeper and more demanding as slowly but inexorably he urged her to him, until they were almost fused as one.

It took a heavy, prolonged thundering on the door to disturb them. 'Is anyone there?' the voice of a night watchman called.

Guy, muttering a swift curse under his breath, rolled to his feet. Alana heard the man say something about someone being seen lurking near the cabins, and Guy explaining tersely that he had been swimming and hadn't put on a light in order not to attract attention.

The man apologised, said he was new on the job and hadn't known.

When he had gone Alana, now on her feet, said tautly, 'I won't bother with a shower. I'll leave straight away.' She could see her jeans on the floor and began pulling them on—then her shirt. Her movements were jerky, but she managed. Guy returned to her. She tried to ignore him but could feel his gaze on her face, fixed moodily.

'I'll see you in,' he drawled. 'There's a private entrance.' He made no mention of anything that had taken place. Evidently he took such romantic interludes in his stride. Which was more than she did! Feeling nearly too shaken to even stand, Alana followed him outside. All was quiet, although a few people were still arriving back from jaunts to other parts of the island.

Because Guy deliberately avoided the better lit paths, she stumbled, and with a sigh he took her arm. 'I suppose you haven't had a chance to become familiar with the grounds.'

Stung, because he must know he was directly responsible, she retorted bitterly, 'That's scarcely my fault.'

He chose to ignore this. 'You haven't seen much of Ischia yet, have you?'

'No,' she replied, more concerned with trying to free her arm. She was grateful for his help, but not for the tremors it was sending through her.

'It's a beautiful island,' he mused. 'Larger than Capri, where Gracie Fields lived.'

'My father remembers her well.'

Guy was mildly reproving, she might have been ten years old. 'She's a bit of a legend for any generation. Doesn't she inspire you to become as famous?'

'No,' Alana replied shortly, unable to understand the

dryness in his voice and still sore about the subject.

As if reading her thoughts, he smiled slightly in the darkness. 'This won't last for ever, you know. You can eventually return to it.'

'After what you told Pascal?'

'No one will have heard of this in London,' he grunted.

Alana raised her eyes in amazement. 'But you said you'd make sure no one ever employed me as a singer again. Milo told me!'

'We'll see,' Guy said curtly, as they entered the hotel.

CHAPTER NINE

ALANA almost confessed she had no intention of continuing with a singing career, once her parents' affairs were in order, but, apart from anything else, she didn't think Guy would be interested. Once out of sight she didn't doubt, as the old saying went, she would be out of his mind. He probably wouldn't care if she sold peanuts on street corners. His lovemaking had shattered her. She had experienced it before, but this evening everything between them had been emotionally intense. Yet the very fact that Guy had been able to walk away as if nothing had happened must prove that for him it had merely been a fleeting diversion.

Before lunch the following day, she rang Milo. It was a remark Ellis Lane had made about being in touch with her agent in London, when Alana returned her bikini, which made Alana wonder why she hadn't thought of contacting London herself. She managed to scrape together sufficient lire, and to her delight it was remarkably simple to get through.

Milo was clearly startled when he answered her call, but she only asked if it were true that Fabian's fiancée was better. When he confirmed that it was, to save him further embarrassment she thanked him and rang off. After speaking to Milo she found herself wondering if perhaps she hadn't been too hasty. If Guy ever discovered what she had done he would be furious that she had doubted his word. He might not understand that it was important she knew for certain that Fabian's fiancée had recovered, that Guy hadn't just been saying so for reasons of his own.

There had been no difference in Guy's general demeanour that morning, he still ordered her around, but she sensed a little more kindness in his eyes and voice when he spoke to her. There was also a hint of tension about him which puzzled her. After lunch he confused her even more by inviting her to visit Porto d'Ischia with him and, although a trifle apprehensive, she accepted and enjoyed herself very much.

Porto d'Ischia was an enchanting resort, with flat-topped Oriental-styled houses climbing steeply up the hillside above the water. Most of the biggest luxury hotels were here, but so cleverly placed and designed they did nothing to detract from the town's appealing beauty. Alana found lots to interest her in the narrow streets which frequently turned into flights of steps and the fifteenth-century castle. She regretted that there wasn't time to visit the small museum or the mineral springs nearby, some of which, Guy told her, reached temperatures near to boiling.

That evening she noticed he dined alone, afterwards disappearing with Pascal into his office. When Ellis Lane swept into the dining-room, as he was leaving, Alana noted, with some satisfaction, that he only acknowledged her with a brief bow.

She slept that night better than she had done for

some weeks, and the next morning had scarcely woken up when she was brought stumbling to her door by a knock which suggested someone wanted to see her on a matter of some urgency. Barely pausing to tie her robe, she was busy pushing her tumbled hair from off her face as she opened the door to find Guy there.

'Why . . .?' Her voice trailed off as she stared at him in surprise. He didn't come to her room any more, and when she was in his suite, as she was for most of the day, he kept his distance. If he wanted to see her in a hurry, he always sent someone else to fetch her. But it wasn't so much that he was here now that momentarily robbed her of her breath. It was the return of the hard, condemning expression on his face, which had been so wonderfully missing yesterday.

'What is it?' she whispered at last, as he continued staring at her with absolute contempt.

When it came to it, he didn't beat about the bush. 'You've been in touch with London?' he snapped.

Now she understood, her heart sank. 'Milo told you?'

'Naturally.'

'I must remember,' she spoke hollowly, 'men have this peculiar thing about sticking together, even when there's no real necessity for it.'

His eyes went icy. 'Don't imagine Milo bothers to inform me of all the tittle-tattle that goes on. If you hadn't rung Fabian as well, I doubt if I'd have heard from him.'

'Fabian . . .?' Her eyes widened in bewilderment. 'Wait a minute! What did you say? Did you say I'd rung Fabian?'

'Please,' Guy cut in roughly, pushing her inside and closing the door as someone came along the corridor, 'I want no more of your lies. Milo rang to inform me that Fabian left the U.K. last night and is on his way here. To find you! And you were the only one who could have let him know where you were. He could arrive any time.'

'I haven't spoken to him!' she protested.

'Shut up!'

Desperately she closed her eyes, trying to think. Opening them again, she blinked up at him dazedly. 'You won't believe me, so I'll not try and convince you, but if it proves anything I'm willing to hide.'

'Oh, no!' he replied furiously, 'I don't go in for amateur dramatics. It's been bad enough so far without making things worse. Everyone on the staff knows you're here, and Fabian is no fool. A few well chosen queries and he'd find it all out. Especially when, with your charming cunning, you'd probably contrive to let him know your exact location within minutes of his entering the hotel.'

'I would promise . . .'

Again he cut her off ruthlessly. 'Promises!' he snapped derisive fingers in her face. 'Yours aren't worth that! No, the only solution is to remove you. Get a case packed and be as quick as you like!'

Where had she heard those words before? Was she going mad? No, Guy was—if he thought she was going to run for ever! 'Listen,' she cried fiercely, her whole body tense from her desire to make him understand, 'if—and I don't really believe it—if Fabian is coming here to declare an undying love for me, what good would he be to your cousin or any other girl? Why not ask yourself that instead of concentrating on another place to hide me?'

'Do you think I haven't asked myself that, Miss Hurst?' he snarled, his face pale under its tan. 'Why should any man want a permanent relationship with a worthless piece of tinsel like yourself? The answer is until the glitter wears off, which we all know doesn't happen overnight. I promised Jane and her parents I'd see that Fabian came to his senses, and I intend giving him one more chance. I'm taking you away and I'll come back in a day or two and talk to him. Now get moving and get dressed, unless you want me to do it for you?'

'Guy!' she made one last appeal. 'Won't you reconsider?'

'No.'

She turned away so he wouldn't see the tears in her eyes. 'Then where are you taking me?'

'You'll find out soon enough.'

Back to London, she supposed, glancing over her shoulder at him helplessly, as she began gathering up her few belongings. When he had informed her curtly that she'd better bring everything, this confirmed her suspicions that this was their destination. Anyway, she concluded, it might only be a waste of time asking again, as any attempt on her part to get through to the grim-faced man beside her seemed doomed to failure. And, in a way, perhaps he was right. She must, as she had thought all along, owe it to Jane to keep out of Fabian's way, as she had no other means of restoring the damage she had done.

They drove to Porto d'Ischia, where only the day before they had spent such a pleasant time. There Guy helped himself to a launch, built on fast though sturdy lines. Alana felt puzzled, as it appeared to be in a private anchorage a little distance from the town.

'Is it yours?' she asked, breaking the cold silence which had existed between them since leaving the hotel.

'Yes,' he replied shortly, 'but a friend looks after it for me and I let him use it for the free maintenance.'

'Why don't you keep it at the hotel?' She had noticed boats anchored by the hotel jetty.

'I'm not often here,' he was working quickly, as though impatient to be off, 'and a boat needs constant attention.'

He might not be here often, but she could see he was no novice when it came to seamanship. Within minutes they were speeding over the blue water of the bay, making for the open sea. The morning air was fresh, and she held her face up to it, drinking it down in deep breaths. Regretfully she watched Ischia receding until it was just a speck on the horizon. She wondered if she would ever see it again. It was a beautiful island and she would liked to have seen more of it.

'Wouldn't it have been quicker to have flown to Naples?' she asked eventually, as the hours passed and they didn't seem to be getting anywhere.

'We aren't going there,' said Guy.

The boat cut through the water. It was a clear, vivid blue. But of course water had no colour at all. It was like life, quite colourless, really, when one stopped being fooled by appearances. Once, not long ago, every time Alana had glanced at Guy Renwick everything had taken on a bright glow. Even on dull days she had found colour everywhere—when she had thought he was growing fond of her.

His brief but confusing statement that they weren't going to the mainland did nothing to remove her depression, but it did startle her. She swung around to him, her blue eyes wide, her lips dry. 'Where are we going, then?'

'To the island, the one I told you about.'

Momentarily diverted, she frowned, 'I didn't take you seriously. You mean you really do own an island?'

'It's not so unusual,' he said curtly. 'Often small ones go for a song. I have another in the Aegean.'

'Greece?'

'Yes.'

Alana sighed impatiently, annoyed with herself for not concentrating on her immediate problems. 'I don't care how many islands you own,' she said fiercely, 'I'm not going to any of them with you!'

'Aren't you?' he enquired silkily.

She refused to recognise defeat, even when it stared her in the face. 'Surely Fabian will guess where you're taking me?'

'No, he won't.'

'Won't Pascal tell him?'

'No,' Guy shook his dark head, 'not a hope.'

'Why not?' she glared at him curiously. 'Why is the Sachs family so loyal?'

Guy altered the course of the boat slightly, his grey eyes concentrating and narrowed. He answered absently, as if his mind was more on what he was doing. 'It's quite simple, really. His family has worked for mine for a couple of generations. We all grew up together.'

'And they still work for you.'

'Most of the time,' Guy replied coolly, slanting her a derisive glance. 'You don't have to be sorry for them, though. There are quite a few of them and they've done very well for themselves. They all have shares in the company and come and go much as they please. Milo spends several months of each year with an uncle of his who's a professor of music in Rome.'

She might have guessed! Hadn't they always seemed as thick as thieves! She would be wise not to look for any help from that source. For the time being all she could do was pretend to give in and perhaps try to find a means of escaping later on.

'How many people live on the island?' she asked, with a view to enlisting their aid.

'None.'

'There—there'll just be the two of us?' Alana gulped and knew it was audible. She felt suddenly frightened. What would being alone together on a lonely island do to her? Even when Guy wasn't touching her she could feel the strong, magnetic force of his body, which seemed to be tuned into exactly the same wavelength as her own. When he so much as glanced at her she could feel it. And while she was usually aware when someone looked at her, only with Guy had she ever experienced an actual physical response. Unhappily she realised that the prickling down her spine, the surge of sensation that rushed through her, was not to be dismissed casually as just one of those things. It only happened with him, and like electricity she recognised the danger. Yet what could she say to him? Any protest on her part would undoubtedly meet with the same reception it had met with so far.

When she heard him confirm mockingly and unrelentingly, 'Yes, there'll only be the two of us,' she merely shook her head. And when he added coldly, 'If you're quite finished asking questions and have nothing better to do, I'd be obliged if you would make me some coffee?' she obeyed him without another murmur.

The island was deserted. Until the moment they arrived Alana had hoped it wouldn't be, but she soon saw that Guy had, in fact, been speaking the truth. He hadn't just been teasing her.

The house might not be as primitive as he had made out, but it was fairly basic. She thought it must once have been two old stone cottages knocked into one and saved from dereliction by some enterprising builder from the mainland. There were four rooms, two bedrooms, a living-room and a kitchen, but only the living-room and one of the bedrooms were sizeable. The bedrooms each contained a bed and a chest of drawers, nothing else, and in the bathroom, Guy had already warned her, there was no hot water. The water was supplied from a spring in the hillside behind the house, and while it was pure and wonderful to drink it was extremely cold.

As he appeared to enjoy telling her this, Alana tried

to take no notice. She being perfectly aware that in his present mood any new discomfort he could find to inflict on her would afford him great satisfaction. He would only be pleased if she protested.

The living-room was furnished with several quite comfortable, wood-framed armchairs, but there was no carpet on the floor, nor any curtains at the windows. The kitchen, too, was bare, with a stone sink, two chairs and a table. The cooking, she was informed, was done by oil as there was no electricity.

'What do we use for lights?' she asked, as he finished showing her round and stood waiting cynically for her withering comments.

When the criticism he obviously expected didn't arrive, he slanted her a suspicious glance. 'Lamps,' he replied curtly.

'I don't appreciate being forced to come here,' she said, as soberly, 'but I think it's nice. In other circumstances I'm sure I could come to love it. I'm not old enough yet,' she assured him coldly, 'to be worrying all the time about my comfort.'

'Just as well,' he snapped, not arguing but looking faintly incredulous.

'What do we eat?' She could see no sign of any food or even a larder. 'I'm not very hungry, but I presume you'll want lunch?'

'I do,' he agreed briefly. 'And I brought some supplies in the boat. This afternoon I'll catch fish for our dinner.'

When he returned from the boat with a couple of laden boxes, she had found a frying-pan and kettle, but that was all.

'I'm afraid you'll have to make do,' he said silkily as she looked askance at him. 'If I left a lot of food and equipment here, passing yachtsmen might be tempted to help themselves.'

'Do many people call here casually?' she enquired,

attempting to conceal the eagerness in her voice.

'It's like looking through a window,' he mocked, 'reading what goes on in your mind. If you're hoping to be rescued, you can forget it. We're too far off the beaten track and the island is too small to attract much interest.'

Alana sighed and decided to concentrate on the supplies he dumped unceremoniously on the table. Cereals, dried milk, coffee, a few tins—she eyed them doubtfully.

'I realise there's not a lot,' he said sharply, 'but we left in a hurry and I didn't want to obviously raid the kitchens and arouse suspicion.'

Did he have to think of everything, even when pushed? 'I wasn't worrying,' she replied flatly. 'Anyway, I never eat much.'

His grey eyes flicked over her. 'You're far too thin. Maybe a spell here won't do you any harm. You look washed out.'

'Well, thank you very much!' she retorted indignantly, her cheeks growing hot, 'I don't suppose it has anything to do with the way you've been making me work these last two weeks?'

Guy merely shrugged broodingly. 'Perhaps I should have taken you to my Greek island. My staff there would soon have fattened you up.'

'You aren't thinking of selling me to some Middle East sheikh,' she jibed, 'as soon as you get some flesh on my bones?'

'I could be thinking more of my own pleasure,' he taunted back, leaving her.

Despite her unfamiliarity with the rather primitive equipment, Alana managed to ignore the disturbed state of her mind and produced a passable meal. While she was busy Guy went around the house opening windows and checking various things. He went to the boat for several more items, including blankets which he deposited on the beds. They ate in comparative silence and afterwards he told her she would have to amuse herself while he went fishing. When she asked why she couldn't come with him, he said she would talk too much and frighten the fish.

She hadn't really wanted to go, she had suggested it because she was sure it would annoy him, yet when he refused her company so curtly, she felt strangely hurt.

When he had gone, she tidied the kitchen and made up the beds. This she supposed he might take as a sign of surrender, but she decided bitterly that she might as well suffer the indignity of imprisonment in comfort. Guy would undoubtedly derive the most satisfaction if she chose to sit in a chair or on the beach all night, rather than go to bed. Besides, she didn't think, for all his jibes, that he would really molest her. His opinion of her was so low she was sure he wouldn't risk getting involved seriously.

Hot and dusty from her efforts, when eventually she finished, she paused to gaze wistfully at the sea. She was tempted to go for a swim. The bathroom, with its huge cast-iron bath and ice-cold water, didn't appeal to her. She had no bikini but could always swim in her panties and bra, which might cover her better than a bikini would.

Hastily collecting a towel, she chose a path in the opposite direction to the one Guy had taken. The island was pretty without being spectacular and she thought she could see why he had chosen it, and why passing boatmen declined to stay. There were no sandy beaches, only a few stony coves, and most people came to this part of the world to stretch out on the sand for hours, in order to acquire a Mediterranean tan.

In one of the coves she stripped her clothes off and swam. Guy was fishing over a mile away, so there was no danger of him coming across her. Nor could there be any danger from the sea, hadn't he remarked over lunch how it was usually as calm as a millpond? While it wasn't quite as smooth as that today, she welcomed its refreshing tang. At least it was removing her oppressive feeling of tiredness. Suddenly invigorated, as the waves became slightly more boisterous, she went farther out and began splashing about.

She was just thinking of turning back when she heard Guy shouting from the shore. Raising her arm, she acknowledged his call but, remembering what she was wearing, decided to wait until he was gone before she went in. Her makeshift suit had seemed fine when she was by herself, but she didn't want him to see her in it.

When she glanced towards the shore again and saw he was no longer there, she began swimming cautiously towards it, watching closely for fear he reappeared. So absorbed was she in looking in this direction, she didn't notice him cutting through the water until he was practically on top of her. Without warning she was grabbed and ordered roughly not to struggle, as he began towing her towards the beach in a life-saving fashion.

Dismay struck Alana as she realised he must have thought she was in trouble and was bent on rescuing her. But when she tried to explain she was all right, he took no notice, if he even heard, and an eddying wave washed into her open mouth, nearly choking her. Another sign he apparently construed as imminent drowning!

Cursing hoarsely under his breath, he flung her on the shore and proceeded to pummel water out of her.

'I—I wasn't in any difficulties!' she spluttered, swallowing sand as the pressure of his hands almost forced her face into it. In a desperate attempt to make him understand, she added, 'Please, Guy, will you get off me!'

His repressive muttering stopped abruptly as he

turned her roughly over. His face was pale with haggard lines of strain and tight anger. 'What do you mean, you weren't in any trouble?' he snapped.

Swallowing hard, Alana stared up at him, as she lay flat on her back. He might not have managed to knock much water out of her, but he had certainly deprived her of her breath. 'I went for a swim,' she managed at last, 'and when you called I waved.'

'Of all the stupid idiots!' he raved. 'I took it you were signalling for help, especially when you didn't move.'

'We must have misunderstood each other,' she faltered, trying to avoid the leaping fury in his eyes. 'I didn't deliberately mislead you.'

'I wonder,' he bit out. 'Some girls will do anything for a bit of fun.'

'You think I'd consider how you pulled me out of the sea—or this—fun?' she exclaimed, as his strong body, bare apart from a pair of ragged shorts, still straddled her.

'There's no accounting for taste,' he said tautly.

Sighing, she decided it might be futile to argue with him. He'd had his mind made up about her long ago, nothing she could say was likely to change it. Suddenly his brief attire made her conscious of how little she had on herself. With quick agitation she became aware of him staring down on her and was reminded of the evening when he had taken her into the cabin by the swimming pool at the hotel.

Having no wish to provoke a repeat of what had happened then, she tried to calm her quickening pulses by asking lightly, 'I have a towel somewhere. I'd be grateful if you could find it for me.'

Instead of decreasing his anger, her deliberately careless tones had the opposite effect. Startling her, Guy rasped, 'You weren't by any chance trying to drown yourself out there?'

'Of course not!' She was horrified to find herself shouting at him. 'We don't all choose the easy way out, like cousin Jane!'

She knew immediately she shouldn't have said such a thing. She wished she could have taken it back, or at least explain that she hadn't meant it, but the quick fury in his eyes allowed her time for none of these things. Pulling her bare body from its sandy bed to meet his halfway, he grasped her tightly. 'You deserve to be punished for that!' he exclaimed furiously.

His lips were cool and tasted of salt as they assaulted her own, as he forced her averted head around and held it still. His knees, digging into the sand on either side of her, made it impossible for her to move. He kissed her deeply, then paused, like an opponent withdrawing a little to tantalise the weaker opposition. While he might have used words to punish her, he had obviously decided a physical reprisal might be much more effective. He had felt her first, brief resistance but had judged when the treacherous vanguard of her emotions had faltered before his more experienced tactics. Now his hand went savagely to her breast and the removal of her bra did nothing to strengthen her increasingly feeble attempts to ward him off. When he crushed her to him again she knew she had lost the battle she had been secretly waging for weeks. Tightly she wrapped her arms around him, incapable of hiding the completeness of her surrender, and for a wild moment she thought he had accepted it. Her blood raced and her heart leaped frantically as their mouths strained together and his hand slid under her to bring the contact of their throbbing limbs even closer.

Then, with a muffled exclamation, which contained more than an element of self-disgust, he wrenched her arms from around his neck and sprang away from her. Without a word of apology he found her towel, dropping it by her side. 'I'll wait,' he said grimly, 'until you get dressed, just in case you feel like playing any more tricks in the sea!'

A few minutes later, when she had numbly done as he ordered and her protesting body was again respectably clad, Alana followed him back to the house. On the way he neither spared her a glance or spoke to her but maintained a discouraging silence. Unable to bear it any longer, she closed her eyes in an attempt to shut out the unrelenting lines of his tall figure. Unfortunately such a practice merely caused her to stumble and only earned her another curt word of rebuke.

At the house, on the kitchen table, lay four good-sized fish. As she stared at them uncertainly, Guy asked briefly, 'Can you cook them?'

'I'm not sure.' She found she couldn't summon the slightest enthusiasm and ignored the impatient tightening of his lips which suggested he had no time for girls who sulked. She didn't bother to explain how it amazed her that he could even think of the fish, let alone contemplate eating them. It proved how little the scene on the beach had really affected him. Here he was, apparently wholly absorbed by thoughts of dinner, while she was so disturbed that even the sight of food sickened her.

'I'll try later,' she assured him dully, pushing past him to her room before she broke down.

Afterwards, when she had washed the sea water from her hair and regained some composure, she returned to the kitchen and made dinner. She baked the fish, which was delicious, as this was the only method she could think of when there was just one ring on which to cook the vegetables. She opened tins of potatoes and peas and made up a packet of white sauce while she frowned over the remaining supplies. There wasn't a lot, they would have to be careful.

If Guy enjoyed his dinner he didn't say so and it

annoyed her that, although he might consider she was directly responsible for their being here, he should take the not inconsiderable struggle she had had to produce such a meal entirely for granted. Yet he looked so tired she didn't protest when he made no offer to help with the dishes but washed up quickly herself while he wandered outside to sit on the moonlit verandah.

After she had finished, Alana made two cups of coffee and took one out to him. He looked lonely and she felt her heart soften with a sudden pity. As always she found herself remembering that, as she refused to tell him all the facts, he couldn't be entirely blamed for thinking the worst of her.

'Would you like me to join you?' she asked tentatively, her mouth softening as she glanced at him more humbly than she had done all day and changing her mind about retiring immediately to her room.

'What for?' he queried so brusquely it was like a slap in the face. 'Do I look in the need of company? Are you offering to comfort me with a few more kisses? Are you hoping that the moonlight is going to make me forget all those which you've squandered on other men? Only a fool like Fabian would ever deliberately touch you.'

Carefully she put down his coffee. She felt so ice-cold she was able to speak with relative calm. 'You've kissed me yourself, both before and after you began hating me.'

'I was amusing myself, nothing more,' he replied curtly. 'What else did you think I'd be doing with a worthless little bitch like you?'

She went so white she was sure he must see it for he was staring straight at her. Her voice cracked as she whispered, 'I thought you were beginning to care for me.'

'You what?' His eyes blazed as if he would liked to have hit her. 'I might admit to a little physical attraction, that's all.'

'For women,' she murmured, almost to herself, 'it can't be one without the other.'

Her small air of desperation appeared to incense him afresh. 'Who do you think you're kidding, darling,' he drawled, with hateful sarcasm. 'Some ladies make a living from it.'

Alana flushed, heat creeping painfully under her clear, delicate skin. 'I wouldn't have anything more to do with you if you p——' In the middle of the word she broke off abruptly, a further wave of embarrassment creeping into her cheeks.

'Paid you?' he sneered, not sparing her. 'Why not come right out and say it? I'm as wealthy as Fabian, and you know it. How much were you going to demand for services rendered that night in the cabin? And don't tell me you wouldn't have gone through with it, when every inch of you was responding. No wonder Fabian was madly infatuated. You'd make even a saint lose his senses!'

'You were going to seduce me?' she whispered, shaking.

'Who was seducing whom?' he laughed mirthlessly. 'I'd be a fool to pretend I didn't want you, but premises which have been used indiscriminately hold little permanent attraction for me.'

'I see.' Tears were rolling down her cheeks now, but she suddenly didn't care if he saw how deeply she was upset and shocked.

'And you can turn off the waterworks,' he rasped unsympathetically. 'I'm too old a hand to be caught by a few tears.'

'I'm sorry.' All the fight had gone out of her. She was dead inside, if the things he said weren't so easily forgotten. Yet, somehow, she was glad he had said them. 'You have to be cruel to be kind, I suppose,' she murmured, again as if talking to herself.

'Now what the hell are you on about?'

'Nothing.' She started, her eyes blank, her small face frozen, the shock his words had imparted spreading to every part of her. 'I thought I loved you, but I don't really feel anything. I expect you killed it all.'

For a moment a white ring formed around his mouth and his hands gently broke the empty coffee cup he was holding. 'Good!' he drawled tightly, taking no notice of the scattered pieces of china at his feet. 'Now, if you've got that off your mind, I'd be much obliged if you'd leave me.'

Alana could smell coffee and bacon next morning when she woke up and stirred uneasily on the point of going back to sleep again. Suddenly realising where she was, she sat up with a start. It was barely daylight and she recalled with a frown how she had been as abruptly awakened, if in a slightly different manner, the previous morning.

Last night she had found it difficult to get to sleep and because Guy was about so early she wondered if he had had the same trouble. He said he visited the island quite frequently, but she doubted if he had ever brought a prisoner before, or even a girl he disliked. He probably found the whole thing so irritating he couldn't rest.

Knowing she wouldn't sleep any more now Guy was up, she got out of bed, washed and dressed and went to the kitchen. He was drinking coffee and eating a piece of toast. He had obviously finished his bacon, but there was more frying in the pan and a tray was set neatly on the table.

Glancing up, his face was no less grim than it had been when Alana had last seen him a few hours ago. He was wearing a pair of cotton shorts with his shirt as yet unbuttoned down the front. The sight of his broad, hair-darkened chest caused her pulse to break into a canter and made her palms feel clammy.

'I was just about to bring your breakfast,' he said, 'before I left. While I'm gone, I'm removing the kerosene from the stove—I don't want you setting yourself on fire. I've filled flasks and there's sandwiches and fruit, which should see you through until I get back.'

Alana's eyes widened with apprehension. What on earth was he talking about? 'Where are you going?' she asked. Then, in a frightened rush before he could answer, 'You can't leave me here on my own, I'm coming with you.'

'No, I'm afraid that won't be possible,' he replied curtly, his eyes fixed on her face so intently, she quivered. There was something different about him, this morning, which she didn't understand. A new grimness, a suggestion that his control wasn't any too good. Which must be nonsense, she mocked herself scornfully. Even if it was partly true and he was uptight about something, wouldn't it take nerves of steel to do what he was doing?

'If you won't take me,' she pleaded, 'surely I can know where you're going?'

'Back to Ischia,' he said briefly, startling her.

'But we've just come from there!' she exclaimed.

'So,' he shrugged, 'what of it? I have to return to discover what Fabian is up to, don't I? And if we're to remain here I shall have to bring more provisions.'

'More provisions?' she stammered unhappily.

'Yes,' he snapped.

'But won't anyone guess,' she didn't mention Fabian by name, 'that I'm with you?'

Guy regarded her flushed cheeks with derisive coldness. 'It wouldn't be the first time a man and woman have been together in a place like this.'

Her eyes were suddenly tormented. 'You—you've had other women here before?'

'No!' He glanced away, as though it angered him

even to look at her. 'And I hope to bring your visit to an end very shortly. That's partly why I'm going to Ischia today.'

CHAPTER TEN

TEN minutes later, Alana watched anxiously as Guy swung his boat away from the jetty with a brief wave of his hand. He would only be gone a few hours, he told her, and, on his way, would call at a neighbouring island and ask a couple who often did work for him to come and stay with her until he got back.

The couple arrived but could speak not a word of English, and as Alana had forgotten to bring her Italian phrase-book she was unable to make them understand she wanted to escape. Or they didn't want to understand, she thought bitterly. They simply laughed at her kindly and went on mending their fishing nets. She didn't even learn their names. They practically ignored her, and when they saw Guy returning they jumped into their boat and were gone.

Alana couldn't recall spending such a long day. No matter what she did, time seemed to drag. It was after seven when Guy tied up at the jetty again, and she saw he wasn't alone. He had a man with him. Even from the house she could see it wasn't Fabian. This man was too fair; his hair was as fair as her own. A startled gasp left her lips and she felt almost faint as she realised incredulously that it was Andrew, her brother!

She never remembered crossing the stony beach, but she must have done, for moments later she found herself enveloped in his bear-like hug.

'Andrew!' she choked, swallowing a sob. 'Oh, Andrew! I can't believe it!'

'I'm sorry, sweetheart,' he groaned, as she buried her damp face against his shoulder while Guy stood grimly watching them. 'No one told me what was going on. I had no idea—the old people said nothing. I got the shock of my life when I discovered you were gone.'

Alana released herself while still holding tight to his arm, as if afraid if she didn't he might disappear. Very conscious of Guy's presence, she tried to pull herself together. 'Andrew,' she murmured, 'I think we should talk privately.'

Andrew said quietly but firmly, 'I think not. Mr Renwick knows all the facts, and if you'd told him everything in the first place you might have spared yourself a lot of anguish.'

'You—you've told him—everything?' Her voice trailing off in startled dismay, she looked at Guy properly for the first time. He met her gaze steadily, although his face was entirely expressionless, and he nodded coldly at the unspoken question in her eyes.

'Yes, I know everything. Why you wanted the money you borrowed from me, and tried to borrow from Fabian, but there are still a lot of other things I don't understand.'

'Neither do I,' she interrupted rather wildly, fearing he was about to probe too deeply. 'You said Fabian was coming, but instead Andrew arrives. And while it doesn't seem impossible that Fabian could have guessed where I was, I'm sure Andrew,' she glanced at her brother, 'couldn't have?'

'No,' Andrew answered quickly, before Guy could intervene, 'it was sheer coincidence. When Mother told me where you were I was alarmed, but not nearly as much as when she added that you'd sent a cheque for five hundred pounds. After that I couldn't get to London quick enough to discover what you were up to. I was at the Remax, playing hell at the reception desk, refusing to believe no one knew where you were, when this chap walks up. I thought it was someone coming to throw me out,' he confessed wryly, 'but he said he knew you and wanted to see you himself, and he thought he knew where you were.'

Alana whispered incredulously, 'You came to Ischia with Fabian?'

Andrew nodded. 'And we thought we'd drawn a blank until Guy appeared this morning.'

'But Fabian isn't with you now?' Alana glanced around uncertainly, as if she expected to find him hidden in the sand.

'No,' her brother smiled at her gently. 'He wanted to find you to apologise for the mess he'd got you into and make sure you were all right. He said that instead of trying to get you to explain why you needed the money, he lost his head and tried to blackmail you. He came to his senses when he believed his fiancée had been seriously injured and he's been desperate to find you and put things right ever since. He didn't know that Mr Renwick believed he was looking for you for an entirely different reason and was hiding you over here.'

'And he's gone home?'

'Yes. Once we got it all sorted out, he decided it might be better. He'll wait and see you in London.'

'What about Mum and Dad?' she whispered bleakly, momentarily forgetting Guy was there. 'They'll still need money. What's going to happen to them, Andrew?'

'Something should,' he said grimly, 'if only because of what they practically forced you to do, as well as making you swear not to tell anyone.'

'I don't think they realised,' she excused them anxiously. 'You know how muddled and confused they get. They never meant to get in debt.'

'Well, I'll take charge now,' Andrew promised

curtly. 'Tally is better, although for a long time it was touch and go, and we're back in the U.K. for good. I've had a terrific T.V. offer which I'd be a fool to turn down. We've actually found a flat in Manchester, although eventually we might have to live in London.'

'Oh, that's wonderful!' Alana smiled, feeling a burden of responsibility already sliding from her shoulders. 'I'm sure if Mum and Dad had a little more time and could sell the house they'd be all right, too.'

'The house is already sold,' Andrew astonished her by proclaiming. 'I was coming to that. A big institution's bought it and the same agent has fixed them up with a nice little villa. What's left, after everything is cleared up, will be invested to give them an income for life. So,' he gave a sigh of satisfaction, 'you can return home whenever you like, love. Mr Renwick will be repaid with interest and, as you never did fancy making a career of singing, you'll be able to train for anything you like.'

Guy broke in while Alana was still groping speechlessly for words. 'I'd like to speak to your sister alone, Andrew, if you don't mind. Perhaps you could go up to the house and put the kettle on?'

'Sure, Guy.' With a quick grin and a nod of his head Andrew left them, and Alana marvelled at the ease with which he and Guy had apparently become friends.

She wanted to go with him, but Guy grasped her hand.

'Please,' he said tightly. 'It won't take long.'

She didn't think he would ever beg, so why did she have a feeling he was near to it? That to speak to her alone was important to him. Her surprise on seeing Andrew had been absolute. Now reaction was setting in, making her shake. She wasn't sure how much more she could take. Nevertheless she went with Guy without a murmur of protest, something stronger than herself keeping her riveted to his side.

A little way along the shore he stopped, still in full view of the cottage where Andrew could quite easily see them. Bewildered, Alana realised that while he apparently wanted to talk to her privately, he didn't intend they should be alone in the physical sense at all.

'I have an apology to add to Fabian's,' he began stiffly, releasing her hand and averting his eyes from her pale but eager face. 'Maybe it wasn't altogether my fault, but I was certainly too quick to jump to the wrong conclusions. About you personally as well as the money you asked for.'

She stood very still, staring at him. His face was a cold, frozen mask and his voice so hard she found it difficult to believe he meant what he was saying.

If she had any doubts, however, he soon swept them aside. 'After Fabian appeared on the scene, I became convinced you were the sort of girl who would do anything for money.'

'Who could blame you?' She had to try and speak lightly. 'As you say, it wasn't entirely your fault you got this impression. I'd made a promise to my parents and felt my hands were tied, but I could have told you more than I did. I just didn't know what to do for the best. Then everything seemed to get in such a muddle, I was sure it was too late to put things right.'

'The fact remains that I misjudged you,' he said harshly. 'Not only that,' he added, staring at her, his eyes chill with anger which she wasn't sure was directed against her or himself, 'I was still willing to believe after we were together in the cabin, when I realised you'd never been with a man before.'

Alana flushed. If he condemned himself it didn't make him like her any more. He was like a stranger. It was painfully clear that having learnt she was inexperienced he had lost interest. The incident on the beach, yesterday, had just been a means of getting rid of his anger. She thought she read embarrassment in his face and shivered.

Bending her head in mute defeat, she whispered unsteadily, 'Please don't let it worry you. It was as much my fault as yours, but no real harm was done. I can easily forget.'

'You can?' His brows rose enigmatically while his eyes darkened. 'So now there's nothing more to be said. Except that I hope you will also forgive me for the way I treated you, on more than one occasion.'

Did he have to drag it out? And how could he ask her forgiveness and sound so savage at the same time? Summoning her last ounce of pride, she managed to nod coolly, 'Please don't think of it again. I assure you I won't.'

On hearing him draw a quick, terse breath, she glanced at him sharply, but his face, though slightly flushed, was still an unreadable mask. His mouth tightened to a cold, hard line and he pushed his hands in his pockets. 'Guy . . .?' she murmured, as for a fleeting moment something in his eyes seemed to contradict this impression.

'Damn you,' he said raggedly, then, as hope flared in her breast, causing her to draw involuntarily closer, he stepped back, away from her. 'Don't let's get sentimental, for God's sake,' he snapped. 'I've had just about enough!'

His words were like a slap in the face and she flinched. As she shrank from him this seemed to only increase his anger. 'Let's get out of here.' His hand came up to grab her arm but he dropped it abruptly, as if reluctant to touch her. 'If we don't get back,' he said brusquely, 'your brother will think I've kidnapped you again.'

The evening which followed wasn't a particularly gay one, but soon after supper Alana announced she was tired and went to bed. During the meal Guy and

Andrew talked, mostly about business and world affairs. Alana, unable to find anything to say because of the terrible weight in her breast, pretended to be busy over the stove as an excuse for not joining in the conversation.

In bed, she cried herself to sleep, and if her eyes were pink and puffy next morning, no one appeared to notice. If ever she did catch Guy's glance, he as quickly looked away.

They left the island early and from Ischia flew to Naples. The journey was exactly the same as Alana had made a few weeks ago, but in reverse. Right up until the last moment she allowed herself to hope, but Guy didn't so much as mention seeing her again. She must have been crazy to imagine he had come to care for her, she told herself, as he said a curt goodbye.

'I'd cut that episode right out of my life, if I were you,' Andrew advised, with an astute glance at Alana's white face as they reached Manchester. 'Guy Renwick's a nice enough chap, but I think you'd be wiser to forget him.'

She thought bitterly, had she any other option, while she nodded at Andrew and said she supposed he was right. 'I'll be all right once I'm home and have something to do.'

'You'll find plenty to do.' Andrew's warm smile approved her spirit even if he still looked slightly anxious. 'You seemed a bit distraught on the island, so I didn't think it was the right time to warn you, but the sale of the house was only completed last week and the old folk haven't actually moved yet. There'll be an awful lot of work even sorting the furniture out.'

'Oh, Andrew, I'm sorry!' She had been so busy thinking of Guy, she'd forgotten about everything else. Now the fact that she was going to have to leave the house where she had lived all her life really began to hit her. The impact wasn't nearly so bad as she'd expected, though, and she wondered desperately why nothing, apart from Guy seemed to matter any more.

'Never mind,' she heard Andrew saying gently, 'it will all get done, eventually. I'll help. I'm afraid Tally's not allowed to take on anything extra because of the baby, but,' he grinned happily, 'she's determined to come and advise!'

Over the next few weeks Alana was grateful that she never seemed to have a moment to think. There was, as Andrew said, roomfuls of furniture to sort and a sale to arrange, for they couldn't possibly take everything with them. The new house, not far away from their old home, was very pleasant, with a large garden. To Alana's astonishment her father took to the garden immediately. It was mostly lawn, but there was a good-sized vegetable patch, together with a small greenhouse.

As they watched him cheerfully cutting the lawn with one of the mowers salvaged from the sale, she couldn't help expressing her surprise, but her mother told her he had always liked gardening but his father would never allow it. He had hired a gardener for them, telling his son it was more dignified.

'Well, this proves it's never too late,' Alana smiled.

'Yes,' Margery Hurst sighed happily, 'it's all working out much better than I ever thought it would.'

Her parents, Alana knew, were eagerly looking forward to their first grandchild. Andrew had found a flat nearby, the bottom half of a huge old Victorian terrace house, which would be ideal for the baby. Tally, his wife, was a lovely girl, already on good terms with her in-laws, who were coming to love her.

Yes, Alana sighed to herself, six weeks later, it was all working out very well, for everyone but herself. She had heard nothing from Guy and instead of getting over him, she found her heartache increasing. It wasn't as if she hadn't tried to forget. Hadn't she worked until she was almost exhausted? And whenever her thoughts

turned to him, she firmly ignored them. All of no avail.
He remained a seemingly permanent fixture in her
heart and mind—so much so that she contemplated a
future without him with a terrible despair.

Then one evening she went to have a last look around
her old home. They still had a key as the furniture sale
had been held on the premises, but tomorrow it would
be handed back to the agent and the new owners would
begin arranging to move in. Apart from a few pieces
of furniture which no one had wanted the whole
place was empty and somehow depressing. Wishing
suddenly she had never come, Alana was running
downstairs to leave when the doorbell rang.

It must be one of the most peculiar sensations, she
thought, to hear a doorbell ringing in a empty house.
Pulling herself together, she ran down the remaining
flight of steps as the bell rang again, impatiently. She
had only known one person who rang and knocked like
that. Again Alana paused, for a moment completely
stunned. But no, it couldn't be! Guy wouldn't know
where to find her. Why did she have to keep thinking
of him? Nearly every day she had to remind herself
there was such a thing as coincidence. If she went on
in this way much longer she could go crazy.

Wholly irritated, she almost ran across the hall and
flung open the door. 'Oh, no!' she cried, before her
voice failed her.

Her eyes wide and dazed met his. How many times
had she found Guy like this on her doorstep? At Mrs
Brice's, in the hotel in London, on Ischia, always
impatiently demanding entrée. It was like seeing a
play over again, and somehow, like a play, she felt it
couldn't be true.

For a moment they stared at each other. Guy was
the first to collect himself. 'May I come in?' he asked
with a slight smile, not greeting her by name either.

The smile, she noticed, didn't quite reach his eyes,

but her own lips wouldn't even attempt a travesty of one. She felt light-headed, peculiar. He had no business coming here, on what was probably a meaningless visit, upsetting her.

'Did you want to see me specially?' she enquired stiffly, at last.

'Yes.' His eyes remained sombre, but with an increasing intentness that alarmed her, Uneasily she felt the familiar prickles under her skin.

'What about?'

'I refuse to discuss it on the doorstep,' he replied tersely.

Detecting a slightly belligerent tone, Alana was unwisely tempted to provoke him. 'I think we've had this argument before.'

'And I certainly don't intend having it again!' He moved so adroitly he was inside, the door closed before she realised what he was doing. Then he was reaching for her and she was left in no doubt regarding his intentions. His arms closed about her like a steel trap while his kiss sent white-hot flames shooting along her limbs as he crushed her lips mercilessly. When the necessity to breathe caused him eventually to lift his head, he still kept a tight hold of her.

'Alana!' he muttered hoarsely, putting her a little distance from him. 'Oh, God, how I've missed you! I intended staying away six months, but six weeks proved my limit. I think I was starting to go mad, quietly but very definitely mad,' he emphasised grimly.

Still completely dazed, she lifted bewildered eyes to his face. He was pale, his mouth tense and strangely white, while his burning gaze seemed to be eating her up. Her swollen lips parted. 'I never thought I'd see you again. How did you know where to find me?'

A savage movement to draw her to him again was halted. 'Andrew gave me your new address. I called and your parents sent me here.' His eyes roved over her restlessly. 'You don't think I would have let you go without it, do you? I've kept in constant touch with him, of course, checking up on you.'

'Andrew never once mentioned it.' She knew a surge of blind anger because of all the unhappiness she had suffered through believing Guy had forgotten.

'I asked him not to,' Guy explained flatly, 'and he agreed you should be given a chance to see things clearly. I knew you felt something for me, but I had to be very sure I wasn't just part of the glitter. The weeks we spent together could scarcely be described as normal,' he added dryly.

'I thought you'd lost interest,' she whispered bleakly.

He smiled ironically, then his eyes narrowed darkly. 'Haven't you missed me?' he demanded suspiciously. 'I took it for granted you had when I saw how thin you'd become, but there could be other reasons. This move, for instance, all the hard work you've done.'

'There's certainly been plenty of that,' she agreed. She would rather he believed she had lost weight because of the move than through pining for him. He said he couldn't stay away, but that didn't necessarily mean he loved her.

The swift grasp he usually had of things was missing. He seemed strangely uncertain as he regarded her, frowning harshly. 'So I could be wrong about other things as well?'

'Quite possibly,' she said coldly.

'I've had a wasted journey!' The fury in his voice lashed her like a whip and her eyes, wide with hurt, flew to his face.

Suddenly she saw the haggard lines of pain on it. There were streaks of grey at his temples and if she was thinner so was he. 'Guy,' she whispered, her voice trembling, 'have you been ill?'

'Yes!' his lips were drawn back from his teeth in a savagely bitter exclamation as he jerked her cruelly to him, 'I've been ill from wanting you, girl, and I still don't know if you give a damn!'

Feeling her mouth crushed once more under the demanding ardour of his, Alana shivered. There was a huge brocade sofa, which its new owner had yet to collect, standing at the back of the hall and Guy carried her to it. He lifted her, without removing his mouth from hers, as if he had already noted its exact position and laid her down on the soft cushions. She felt the weight of his heavy body descend beside her. Then he was holding her tightly, his lips forcing hers apart as their mutual passion mounted and flared, like a spark set to kindling.

Alana had tried to keep her response lukewarm, common sense telling her she should know a lot more about how he actually felt before she let him guess the depth of her own feelings, but there was a desire, a need within her she couldn't fight. With a small moan her arms went round his neck and she clung to him. Without reserve she gave herself to him, her pulses racing as she felt his body tremble in response.

His searching hands were on her waist, slowly easing her shirt from her jeans, unbuttoning it insidiously before dealing likewise with her silky bra. Then he caressed her rounded breasts while his kisses grew more passionate and his body hardened with an impatient urgency he made no attempt to conceal.

The effort it took to regain control was explicit in his muttered curse. Not trusting himself another moment, he withdrew with a smothered groan. 'I want you,' he said thickly, his eyes blazing darkly.

'Just—want?' Tears dampened Alana's feverish cheeks, as she came back to earth with a bump and tried hastily to cover herself up.

He wouldn't allow it. Catching her groping hands,

he held them prisoner above her head and stared at her hungrily.

'Want—love?' he grated savagely, his eyes touching every part of her with fire. 'What's the difference? If love is wanting someone until it becomes a pain impossible to live with, then I love you. But want has to be part of it too, what would one be without the other?'

'You're sure?' she whispered, her voice catching huskily in her throat.

'Sure?' His mouth contorted with harsh pain. 'It has to be love. What else would you call it? This craving desire for one special girl, night and day. Wanting to be with her in sickness and in health. Even able to envisualise her when she's old and grey and knowing the feeling, the burning love you have for her will never fade.'

Alana gulped, so shaken by what he was saying, she could only stare at him mutely, She wasn't aware of the hurt in her blue eyes fading as a wondering glow took its place. A radiance which told the waiting man all he was so desperately anxious to know.

'Say it,' he muttered tersely, his hard cheeks colouring a dull red.

'Need I?' she breathed, the fleeting brush of his lips sending a fever burning along her veins. She wanted to touch his face lovingly with her hands, to let them help her express the love she had for him, but as he still held her fast she had to allow her eyes to do it for her.

'Don't play with me,' he warned, his body tense, his eyes inflamed by the force of his feelings.

'Oh, Guy!' as he suddenly released her, she buried her head against his broad shoulder, 'I've loved you for so long it's been a torment. That last evening, on the island, when you were like a stranger, I thought I'd never be happy again. I wanted to tell you I loved you then, but you were so horribly distant I couldn't find the courage. You were the same on the journey home, which was why I was sure you had no special feeling for me, one way or another.'

Instead of lightening, the dark mask of his face tightened. 'Don't remind me of that,' he groaned. 'There was such a lot I wanted to explain but couldn't. If I had,' he said grimly, 'I could never have let you go. I had to keep it to the bare essentials while I really wanted to get down on my knees. When I learnt the truth from Andrew and Fabian on Ischia, I got the shock of my life, but I think deep inside me I'd always known. If I'd been completely honest I would have challenged some of the not very convincing explanations you gave.' His mouth twisted in wry self-derision. 'I believe I deliberately used the tales you told me, when you were trying to borrow money for your parents, in order to prevent myself getting more deeply committed than I already was.'

Alana sighed, protestingly. 'It wasn't your fault. You had to believe the worst, after what I did.'

'That's just the point. I shouldn't have believed it!' he groaned aloud, ruffling her bright hair. 'When I first met you, on the train, I saw you as an innocent young girl. That wasn't why I was immediately attracted, though. As soon as I looked at you, I was conscious of something I'd never felt before. I tried to ignore it, but the feeling grew. I didn't understand it, then I refused to even try to, but I felt I was being taken over by something over which I had no control. By the time we reached London I was concentrating on only one thing—making sure I was going to see you again.'

As Alana's thoughts went back to that momentous night, her mind swung unsteadily. 'Do you usually travel by train? After I discovered who you really were, I always meant to ask you.'

'No,' Guy shook his head, his hand moving restlessly over her face, pausing on her shoulder, 'I'd been looking over hotel sites, travelling by car. The initial survey is still something I like to do myself, and to do it by car is the only way. At least I think so. I can take my time, see what the surrounding countryside had to offer. On this occasion, however, my car broke down. I could have hired another or caught a plane, but as I was near a station, on sudden impulse I hopped on a train.'

'I still think you should have told me the truth about yourself before you did,' she pouted.

A hint of a teasing smile touched his sombre expression. 'I know, my sweet, but you were an obstinate little cuss, even then. I swear I didn't find it easy to deceive you, but I was convinced if you knew I was rich you would think I was only out to amuse myself and would refuse to see me again. I could sense your prickly pride a mile off.'

'Would it have mattered then if I'd refused to see you again?'

The faint smile died from his face as he snapped curtly, 'Don't joke about it, Alana. I'm not in the mood.' He paused, his hands tightening on her slender frame as he gazed at her intently. 'Try to understand. I was falling in love, which I'd thought would never happen to me, and I was willing to resort to almost anything to make sure you stayed in my life.'

Alana's lashes flickered at the turbulent passion she saw in his eyes. 'This was why you offered me a job at the Remax?'

'Yes, and when Milo said you were good I believed in fate again.'

'What were you going to do if I couldn't sing?' she enquired dazedly.

'Find you something else, or abduct you,' he growled. 'I was quite ready to do something drastic.'

'But you'd only known me a few hours,' she frowned incredulously. 'I never guessed.'

'You weren't meant to,' he muttered darkly. 'All the same, you must have had some idea, especially after I'd taken you out and kissed you.'

She flushed and confessed. 'I suppose I was too busy trying to hide my own feelings. Everything seemed to be happening too quickly, and I thought what you felt for me was just—just sex.'

'That did come into it,' his mouth twisted wryly as he bent to kiss the pale, exposed curves of her breasts. 'I was jealous of every man who looked at you. When you were singing I saw the lust on their faces and hated every man in the room.'

As the fire which the touch of his lips evoked whipped through her she drew a quick breath. 'Not half as much as I hated Mrs Templeton!'

'Veronica?' As his head came up reluctantly, his smouldering glance revealed a hint of satisfaction at her undisguised jealousy. 'Did you really, darling? There was never anything between us. I had no idea she was coming to London, or that she would talk of the engagement party I was giving for Jane and Fabian as something I'd asked her to arrange. Fabian confessed it was he who told you I'd spent the weekend with her at the cottage, but it wasn't true, and when you accused me of womanising I was so furious I couldn't bring myself to explain.'

Alana's eyes held more than a hint of regret, too. 'If only I could do it all over again,' she whispered ruefully, 'I wouldn't make the same mistakes.'

'Nor I,' Guy muttered thickly. 'I was in too much of a hurry, but I felt sure you were coming to care for me. Then, when you were so furious about my deception over my name, I decided that any love between us had existed only in my imagination and was best forgotten. I'm afraid,' his mouth quirked in a dry grin, 'you hurt my pride considerably, you little madam, and I believed I was well rid of you.'

To Alana's horror tears pricked the backs of her eyes and she had some difficulty stopping them from overflowing. Seeing Guy's quick concern, she laughed shakily. 'It's because I still remember how utterly miserable I was. I know I said a lot of things I didn't mean, that evening, but I was so distraught through loving you so much, I scarcely realised what I was saying. Afterwards, when you were so nasty to me, I just wanted to die.'

'Forgive me.' He kissed her, this time his lips gentle and comforting. 'That was the outraged pride I mentioned. I intended to punish you, but you must have noticed I couldn't keep away from you. I was on the verge of burying my pride and having a frank talk with you when I discovered you were trying to borrow money from Fabian. I felt I'd had enough. Jane was heartbroken and for her sake, as well as mine, I had to get rid of you. And Ischia seemed the best idea I could come up with. Sacking you, leaving you free to wander around London, would only be playing into Fabian's hands.'

'So you arranged, with Milo's help, to banish me?' she sighed.

'I more or less forced him to do what he did, but he was far from willing,' Guy admitted remorsefully. 'Even now I don't think he's forgiven me. It seems strange, doesn't it,' he added bitterly, 'that all along Milo believed in you while I, who loved you, didn't?'

'Perhaps that was why.' Alana's eyes softened with a wiser understanding. 'I discovered for myself how full of doubts love can make one. Why did you follow me to Ischia?' she asked suddenly.

'Because I decided banishing you wasn't such a good idea after all. There was the possibility of Fabian finding out where you were and following. So I convinced

myself I ought to go and keep an eye on you, teach
you a final lesson. Who was fooling who, I wonder?'
he murmured wryly. 'On Ischia I meant to make your
life hell, but it was my own life that became that. I
clung to Ellis Lane like a drowning man clings to a
straw, until I think she guessed about you. Taking you
to my own small island was the final mistake. After I
thought you were drowning, and I kissed you on the
beach, I knew I couldn't stay. If I had done I couldn't
have kept my hands off you. I was going to find some
means of getting you away.'

Alana murmured slowly, lowering her heavy lashes
so he couldn't see the reflection of remembered pain.
'I thought you hated me.'

'And now you know how much I love you,' he said,
his voice so full of warmth and tenderness, her eyes
jerked back to his face. 'Come on, my sweet,' he placed
his fingers gently under her chin, noting her trembling
lips. 'If talking's doing this to you,' he told her softly,
'I'll have to try something else! I'll only ask one more
thing. How soon will you marry me?'

He spoke so impatiently, her heart began to race.
'As soon as you like,' she whispered shamelessly.

A fierce glimmer of triumph lit his eyes until passion
darkened them. 'Tomorrow?' he demanded huskily.
'I've had the necessary arrangements made for weeks.
It was the one thing which kept me sane, the hope that
you would say yes. I'd marry you tonight,' he threatened, 'but, because of your family, I might just manage
to wait another twelve hours or so.'

When she nodded, helplessly adoring, he gathered
her urgently closer, devouring her with kisses, his
mouth seeking and finding hers as if he was already
possessing her. Fiercely she clung to him, letting the
expertise of his caressing hands on her skin arouse her
until she was conscious of nothing but drifting on a
rising tide of sheer ecstasy. Coherent thought left her

mind as his mouth moved lower, whispering her name as he kissed her throbbing flesh in a way that both tantalised and excited her. She could hear the thudding of his heart above hers, the gasping of his breath as her own heart began to race and she returned his kisses passionately.

A moment later he drew away from her. 'If I don't stop now it will be too late,' he said hoarsely.

Her body still clamouring for his, Alana gazed at him numbly. 'Would it matter—if we love each other?'

'Not to me.' His sensual mouth tightened in an obvious effort to retain the control he had achieved over his desire for her. 'But to you it might. That's why I'm refusing to take the risk, even though I'm having to suffer.'

'Until tomorrow, then,' she swallowed.

'That's a promise, you little minx,' Guy growled threateningly, his eyes alive with a warm sexuality which made her steadying pulse quicken again. Before she could find the breath to reply, he went on, 'I hope you aren't thinking of continuing with your singing, or taking up some other career, after we're married?'

'Don't you want me to work?' she teased.

'I do not!' If he tried to keep his answer light, the thickness of his voice betrayed him. 'After we're married I want you to want only me, and my children.'

She trembled visibly but managed to ask, in the same tone she had just used, 'Will it be a full-time job, sir?'

'One for life,' he replied solemnly. 'But I can assure you the rewards will be great.'

Her eyes met his with an increasing glow. Suddenly throwing her arms around his neck, she buried her face in his throat. 'I only want your love,' she cried fiercely, 'nothing else.'

'Then I'll have to make sure you get enough.' His voice deepened, deliberately teasing, as he began softly kissing her again. 'If you promise to pay me back with interest, sweetheart, I'm sure you'll find nothing to complain about.'

Alana blushed as passion replaced the mocking glint in his eyes and his mouth hovered, leaving the initiative to her expectantly. 'Of course,' she murmured, and as she proceeded to do this straight away, the only response she received was a groan of pleasure.

A WORD ABOUT THE AUTHOR

Margaret Pargeter's earliest memories are of her childhood in Northumberland, in northern England. World War II was raging, but in spite of the gravity of the times, she recalls, people always tried to find something to smile about. That memory, and that philosophy, have stayed with her through the years.

Short-story writing was a habit that began in her early teens, and after her marriage she wrote serials for a newspaper. When her children were in school she did several years of market research, which she believes gave her a greater insight into people and their problems, insight that today helps her in creating interesting plots and developing believable characters.

Today, Margaret lives in a small house in the quiet Northumbrian valley where she grew up. On the subject of writing romances, she is convinced of one thing: "It is not easy. But not the least among my blessings is the pleasure I get from knowing that people enjoy reading my books."

Legacy of
PASSION
BY CATHERINE KAY

A love story begun long ago comes full circle...

Venice, 1819: Contessa Allegra di Rienzi, young, innocent, unhappily married. She gave her love to Lord Byron—scandalous, irresistible English poet. Their brief, tempestuous affair left her with a shattered heart, a few poignant mementos—and a daughter he never knew about.

Boston, today: Allegra Brent, modern, independent, restless. She learned the secret of her great-great-great-grandmother and journeyed to Venice to find the di Rienzi heirs. There she met the handsome, cynical, blood-stirring Conte Renaldo di Rienzi, and like her ancestor before her, recklessly, hopelessly lost her heart.

Take these 4 best-selling novels FREE

Harlequin Presents...

Take these 4 best-selling novels FREE

 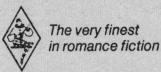